THE
DESTINATION

by Ryan Kaminski

THE DESTINATION

SPECIAL NOTE

Anyone receiving permission to produce THE DESTINATION is required to give credit to the Author as sole and exclusive Author of the Play on the title page of all programs distributed in connection with performances of the Play and in all instances in which the title of the Play appears for purposes of advertising, publicizing or otherwise exploiting the Play and/or a production thereof. The name of the Author must appear on a separate line, in which no other name appears, immediately beneath the title and in size of type equal to 50% of the size of the largest, most prominent letter used for the title of the Play. No person, firm, or entity may receive credit larger or more prominent than that accorded the Author.

SPECIAL NOTE ON SONGS AND RECORDINGS

For performances of copyrighted songs, arrangements or recordings mentioned in these Plays, the permission of the copyright owner(s) must be obtained. Other songs, arrangements or recordings may be substituted provided permission from the copyright owner(s) of such songs, arrangements or recordings is obtained; or songs, arrangements or recordings in the public domain may be substituted.

Book Design: Jonathan Cook
First Edition: March 2024
ISBN: 978-1-7375216-8-6

"For my parents, grandparents, and wife, thank you all for always believing in me."

THE DESTINATION

CHARACTERS

MARILYN MORRIS
Aspiring novelist. Daughter of a minister. Running from a dark past while trying to recover from a serious addiction. Early 30s.

ARTHUR NELLIGAN
Motel Proprietor. Articulate and refined with a Southern drawl. Appears old and decrepit at beginning of play but gradually becomes younger as the play progresses. Late 30s in his youngest form.

GRETCHEN HUNTER
Former ballerina turned wife of a politician. Has embraced the wealth her marriage has brought her. Early 50s.

TOM GAVIN
Younger brother of a successful thief. Desperate to forget the abuse he has endured in life. Mid-30s.

THE STRANGER/VOICE ON RADIO
Female. Former associate of Arthur's. Appears youthful at the beginning of the play but gradually becomes older as the play progresses. Early 30s in youngest form.

PLACE
The Nelligan Motel.

TIME
The night of December 21st through the early morning hours of January 1st. Present day.

ACT ONE
Scene 1

The lounge of the Nelligan Motel.

Nighttime.

Next to the front door is a coat rack where a red suit and a black tie hang. There are two elevator doors in the room with a vintage radio between them. A door to an offstage hallway is next to a check-in counter where a notebook, pen, and bell rest atop the surface. In the corner of the room is an armchair, a small stand, a trash can, and a glass cage atop a table. A red cloth covers the cage. Also in the room are chairs, a couch, and a coffee table with a bowl of fruit atop its surface. In another corner of the room rests a bar cart which is also covered by a red cloth.

At rise, a blizzard rages outside. The sound of feet trudging through the snow is heard followed by a series of knocks on the front door.

TOM. *(Offstage.)* Oh, for the love of …! *(The front door opens, and Tom Gavin, Gretchen Hunter, and Marilyn Morris enter. Tom carries a trunk and wears a heavy coat. Gretchen wears a fur coat and carries a designer suitcase and pocketbook. Marilyn wears a flimsy jacket and carries a purse, beat-up satchel, and a suitcase. Their appearances should indicate they got caught in the storm.)* You don't need to knock. It's a motel.

GRETCHEN. And how do you know that, may I ask?

TOM. There was one of those vacancy signs out front.

GRETCHEN. *(Examines the lounge.)* All right, so this is a motel. A rather unkempt motel … *(Gestures to red cloths.)* Wait. Why is everything covered up? *(To hallway door.)* Hello? Is anybody here? HELLO!?

TOM. *(Covers ears.)* Geez! You can't just scream like that. You need to go up to the front desk and ring for assistance. Like so … *(He approaches the front desk and rings the bell.)* YO! ANYBODY HERE!?

GRETCHEN. *(To Marilyn.)* Real scholar that one. *(Nods to trunk.)* I sensed it the moment he got on the bus lugging around that monstrosity.

TOM. *(Looks around counter.)* No phone, no computer. Not even a cash register. Whoever's in charge here is stuck in the Stone Age or something. You girls have any idea what this place is called?

GRETCHEN. Excuse me. Girls? We are women.

TOM. All right. Either of you women know the name of this damn place?

GRETCHEN. Well, I never …

MARILYN. The Nelligan Motel. There was a plaque above the doorway.

TOM. Nelligan Motel, huh?

GRETCHEN. *(Pulls out cell phone.)* I could barely see two inches in front of me out there. *(Examines screen.)* Oh no. I don't have any cell service. *(Tom and Marilyn instinctively pull out their own cell phones and examine their screens.)*

MARILYN. Me neither.

TOM. Nope. Son of a …

GRETCHEN. This cannot be happening. I cannot, I will not, spend my Christmas stuck at some sleazy, abandoned motel.

MARILYN. I don't think this place is abandoned. Right before we got off the bus, I saw a woman in a white dress out front.

GRETCHEN. You saw what? Why on earth would a woman in a white dress be walking around outside in the middle of a blizzard?

MARILYN. The blizzard did come out of nowhere. Maybe she's a guest here and got caught in it like we did.

TOM. So, where is this girl … *(Catches Gretchen's stare.)* … I mean, woman, now?

MARILYN. Maybe she's in one of the rooms?

GRETCHEN. Well then, she's either deaf or just plain clueless. *(To hallway door.)* HELLO! HELLO, CAN YOU HEAR US!?

MARILYN. Let's think about this for a second. The front door was open. The lights are on … *(Wipes her forehead.)* … and the heat's on too. Someone else is obviously here. While we wait for them, why don't we hang up our coats and sit down? My father would always have people sit down when they came to see him. He'd say, "most of the time, your problems don't seem all that bad when you're sitting down." He was usually right. *(She crosses to the coat hanger. Gretchen follows. Tom slips the pen at the counter into his pocket. Marilyn hangs up her coat and notices the suit and tie.)* See? I told you we're not alone.

GRETCHEN. *(Examines tie and suit.)* Whoever else is here certainly has an appreciation for the finer things in life. *(She hangs up her coat. Tom reaches the coat hanger and hangs up his coat next. He looks over the coffee table and notices the bowl of fruit. He sits on the couch and picks up a grape.)*

TOM. They're real. *(Eats the grape.)* And fresh. Very fresh.

MARILYN. *(Gestures to radio.)* How's about I see if I can

get that to work?

GRETCHEN. Try to find a weather report. *(Marilyn sets down her purse and satchel on the seat next to Tom. She then crosses to the radio and fiddles with the dials. Gretchen crosses to the front door and creaks it open. She stares outside. When Tom is certain neither woman is watching, he reaches into Marilyn's purse and takes out some money. He puts the money into his pocket.)* It's like the end of the world out there. You can't even see our bus. *(Tom continues to rummage through the purse. He finds a tourniquet. He stares at Marilyn upon making his discovery.)*

MARILYN. I think I got something. *(The radio springs to life prompting Gretchen to close the front door. Tom shoves the tourniquet back into the purse.)*

VOICE ON THE RADIO (V.O) …stay tuned for a report at the top of the hour. *(Some instrumental Christmas music begins to play. Marilyn gets ready to change the station.)*

MARILYN. I guess we'll have to tune in later.

GRETCHEN. Oh, leave it on. 'Tis the season after all. *(She hums to herself as she sits in one of the chairs. Marilyn scoops up the satchel and sits. She opens the satchel and looks inside. She breathes a sigh of relief and sets it down. Unbeknownst to any of them, the elevator doors open, and Arthur Nelligan enters. He walks with a walker. The elevator doors close behind him.)* Everything all right?

MARILYN. Yeah. Just making sure nothing got wet on the inside. *(She dabs at her forehead. Tom notices something beneath her sleeve.)*

GRETCHEN. So what did your father do for a living? You said people would come to see him about their problems. Was he a psychiatrist?

MARILYN. Oh, no, he was a minister.

GRETCHEN. How nice! And what do you do?

MARILYN. Um … I'm kinda unemployed at the moment but I'm hoping to … *(Arthur turns off the radio. Marilyn, Tom, and Gretchen turn and finally notice him.)*

ARTHUR. Oh, hello! I was down in the basement when I heard the music. I'm sorry. I didn't mean to frighten y'all.

GRETCHEN. We're the ones who should be apologizing. I hope we didn't frighten you.

ARTHUR. I tell ya, if that storm out there doesn't frighten me, nothing will. Heck, if it was rain instead of snow, we'd all be building arks right now. *(Looks them over.)* Did you three drive out here, or did someone drop you off?

TOM. We were on a bus, and our driver …

GRETCHEN. Don't get me started on that man. One of the most infernal people I've ever met. Late to pick us up, rude as can be, and when the blizzard began to pick up, he swerved straight off the road!

ARTHUR. And where is this infernal driver now?

GRETCHEN. That's the best part. He abandoned us!

TOM. He flagged down some passing driver and hitched a ride. That was when we saw the lights to this place.

ARTHUR. Well, I'm glad you did. It's gonna be bad all night.

GRETCHEN. All night? You mean we're going to be stuck … here?

ARTHUR. I'm afraid so. Of course, if paying for a room is an issue, we can certainly negotiate.

GRETCHEN. No, it's not that. My sister-in-law is waiting for me in Pittsburgh, and I haven't been able to call her.

ARTHUR. I'm afraid cell service avoids this place like one of the Egyptian plagues. I'd let you use the landline, but the storm knocked it out a few minutes ago. I know it's not the news y'all wanted to hear, but hopefully things will turn round in the morning. *(Begins to cross over with his walker.)* Until then, try to relax and make yourselves at home. I'll be over to assist as soon as I can.

GRETCHEN. Please. Let us assist you. *(She rises and crosses over to him. She helps him as he walks to one of the chairs. She then retakes her seat.)*

ARTHUR. Thank you. I know I may not look it now, but I am expected to make a full recovery. *(Sits down.)* Now, I believe some introductions are in order. My name is Arthur Nelligan. I'm the proprietor of this establishment.

TOM. The Nelligan Motel. Name of the place makes sense now.

ARTHUR. Y'all must forgive me for its current state. *(Gestures to coverings.)* You three are the first guests I've had in quite a while.

MARILYN. What about the woman?

ARTHUR. I beg your pardon.

MARILYN. The woman in the white dress. I saw her walking towards the front door right before we swerved off the road.

ARTHUR. I'm afraid you're mistaken, sweetheart. There's no one else here. If there was, I'd know.

MARILYN. That can't be right. I swear … I saw … *(Her body shakes. She touches her forehead only to find more perspiration. She rises, clutching her stomach.)* I'm not feeling well. Is there a bathroom I can use?

ARTHUR. *(Gestures to hallway door.)* Sixth door on the left. *(She rushes to the hallway door and exits.)* Poor girl. Must've been an especially rough bus ride. *(To Gretchen.)* So, are you a nurse?

GRETCHEN. A nurse?

ARTHUR. Given the way you've been tending to my needs

and helping me about the place, I was just wondering …

GRETCHEN. Oh, no, not at all. The last job I worked, believe it or not, was as a ballerina. *(Gestures to her body.)* As you can imagine, I haven't worked in quite a while. I have had experience helping people with walkers because my husband had one. My name's Gretchen. Gretchen Hunter. *(She outstretches her hand. Arthur shakes it.)*

ARTHUR. Gretchen Hunter. Where have I heard that name before? *(Thinks.)* Goodness gracious. Was your husband the mayor of Pittsburgh?

GRETCHEN. He was. A long time ago.

ARTHUR. Well, I'll be. I was so saddened to hear about his passing. I know he had been ill for many years.

TOM. Are we talking about Chuck Hunter? The same guy who fell down the stairs and cracked his head open? *(No response.)* I didn't mean for it to come out like that. I was thinking out loud.

ARTHUR. *(To Gretchen.)* I think what our friend here is trying to say, is that the deaths that hurt us the most, are usually the ones caused by the simplest of things.

TOM. Yes. That's what I meant. *(To Gretchen.)* I'm sorry for your loss. Really, I am.

GRETCHEN. Thank you. What did you say your name was again?

TOM. Tom. *(He leans over to shake Gretchen's hand only to realize he has grape juice on his palm. He rubs it off on the side of his pants. And then apologetically to Arthur …)* I'm sorry. I saw the grapes on the table and figured…

ARTHUR. No apology needed. Try one of the apples. Go on. *(Tom takes an apple and bites it. Arthur rises with his walker.)* We've got plenty to eat and more than plenty to drink. *(He pulls off the cloth at the bar cart. He grabs a bottle.)* How's about a hard cider to go with that apple?

(Tom nods. Arthur hands him the bottle.) What about you, Gretchen? You seem like the kind of woman who appreciates the finer things in life. How's about a nice glass of brandy?

GRETCHEN. I would love one. *(Arthur pulls out a bottle and pours her a glass. He notices Tom stares at the apple.)*

ARTHUR. Everything okay, Tom? Not finding any half-eaten worms in there, I hope.

TOM. Nah, it's just … when I was a kid, my brother and I lived with our grandfather down in the Louisiana swamp. Now and then, he'd send us into town to get apples. This tastes exactly like one of the apples we'd get for him.

ARTHUR. While I did spend some time in New Orleans a while back, I certainly didn't bring up any produce with me if that's what you're implying.

TOM. No. It's just … strange. *(He takes another bite. Marilyn reenters from the hallway.)*

ARTHUR. *(To Marilyn.)* Hi, sweetheart. You feeling any better?

MARILYN. Not really. I'm gonna sit over here for a bit. *(She sits in the armchair. Tom sets down his apple.)*

TOM. Hey, do you have anything non-alcoholic, Mr. Nelligan? *(Nods to Marilyn.)* For her.

ARTHUR. Yes, of course. *(Arthur pulls out a water bottle from the bar cart. He hands it to Tom and then takes a seat near Gretchen.)*

GRETCHEN. *(To Arthur.)* So, you mentioned visiting New Orleans. What other cities have you been to? *(Tom takes the water bottle with one hand and picks up his cider with the other. He crosses to Marilyn. He hands her the bottle.)*

MARILYN. Thank you.

TOM. Mind if I join?

MARILYN. Go right ahead. *(Tom takes one of the chairs and places it beside her. He sits.)* I'm just a little nauseous. *(Wipes mouth.)* I think it was all those bus fumes.

TOM. Look, you don't need to pretend in front of me. I saw the tourniquet in your purse. And I saw the needle marks on your arms … *(She starts to rise. He stops her.)* Please. I'm not here to judge. I know what you're going through. We can talk if you want. *(Marilyn settles back in the armchair. Tom opens the water bottle for her.)* When was the last time you used?

MARILYN. Three days ago.

TOM. You're trying to quit cold turkey? Must be awful.

MARILYN. Especially when you imagine seeing ladies in white dresses outside in the middle of a blizzard. I'm sorry did you say you knew what I was going through?

TOM. Not personally, but back in high school I had a … friend whose mom used. Got so bad she started shooting up in the school parking lot at dismissal one day. Naturally every kid saw. I'll never forget what it was like for my friend after that. Sometimes when we had a place to ourselves, we'd just lie in the bedroom together for hours because it was too painful to even move. What I'm trying to say is, don't give up. Don't give up because although it may not seem like it now, you're not the only one who's suffering.

MARILYN. *(Sips some water.)* So … what was her name?

TOM. Whose name?

MARILYN. Your friend. It's obvious you were in love with her. I may be going through a lot right now, but I'm not clueless.

TOM. *(After a long sip of cider.)* Sam.

MARILYN. Well then, this Sam was a lucky girl to have a guy like you in her life. I hope she didn't blow it. *(Tom smiles. At the couch, Gretchen and Arthur finish their conversation.)*

GRETCHEN. I'm impressed, Mr. Nelligan. It sounds like you've been just about everywhere.

ARTHUR. *(Gestures to his legs.)* Well, here's hoping these old things will heal sooner rather than later so I can get back to travelling again. *(Rises with walker.)* How's about I get y'all checked in for the night? *(He crosses to the front desk. Gretchen collects her things and follows. She has difficulty staying balanced. Arthur notices.)* Everything alright?

GRETCHEN. Just a little tipsy. *(They continue to the counter. Arthur walks behind it and turns the notebook around so it faces her. He briefly looks for the pen before he pulls out a new one so that Gretchen can sign in. Back at the armchair, Tom sets down his cider and helps Marilyn to her feet. They cross to the coffee table. Tom carries back his chair while Marilyn collects her things.)* I guess that brandy hit me harder than I thought. *(A realization hits her.)* Oh no. Before I got on that bus, I took a little something to help with this diet I'm on. I'm really not supposed to mix it with alcohol. *(Marilyn examines the contents within her satchel. Tom crosses back to the armchair and picks up his cider. He hears hissing coming from the cage covered by the red cloth.)*

ARTHUR. *(To Gretchen.)* You're probably just feeling the booze on an empty stomach. How's about I whip you up a nice Southern breakfast in the morning?

GRETCHEN. Sounds wonderful.

ARTHUR. *(Hands her a key.)* Room number one on the right. Have a good night, Gretchen.

GRETCHEN. You too, Mr. Nelligan. *(She exits out the hallway door. Tom pulls off the cloth to reveal a glass cage filled with snakes.)*

TOM. *(Surprised by the sight.)* What the …?

ARTHUR. Ah. I see you discovered my little collection.

TOM. Little? Those snakes don't look so little to me.

MARILYN. Snakes?! *(She spins around and drops her satchel at the sight. A collection of loose-leaf papers, scrap papers, and even some napkins spill onto the floor. Tom crosses over to Marilyn and begins to help her pick up the papers.)*

ARTHUR. Oh my. I guess I should've warned y'all about what was under that cover. *(Off their reactions.)* I assure you, they're completely harmless. I can take one out and show you.

MARILYN. *(Avoids looking up.)* No. I'm … I'm afraid of snakes. *(Arthur reaches into the cage. Several angry hisses are heard.)*

ARTHUR. There's no reason to be. I promise he won't bite.

MARILYN. *(Avoids looking up.)* I said I'M AFRAID! *(A moment passes. Tom hands her the rest of the fallen papers. She puts them into the satchel only to have her hand tremble.)* Look, I didn't mean to yell. I just haven't been feeling myself tonight. I'm sorry.

ARTHUR. I'll meet you at the counter. *(He crosses behind the counter. Marilyn approaches from the front. Tom collects his trunk.)*

MARILYN. Ever have one of those days you wish you could start over?

ARTHUR. Too many to count. While we certainly can't redo a day, there are certain aspects about it that we can redo. Take introductions for instance. *(Outstretches hand.)* Welcome to the Nelligan Motel. I'm Arthur Nelligan.

MARILYN. *(Smiles and shakes his hand.)* Marilyn Morris.

ARTHUR. Pleased to meet you, Marilyn Morris. *(Hands her pen.)* Were you able to collect all your papers?

MARILYN. *(Signing in.)* I think so.

ARTHUR. What are they? Business documents? *(Jokingly.)* Love letters from some clodhopper who couldn't take a hint.

MARILYN. Actually they're pages to a novel I wrote.

ARTHUR. A novel? My, my, my. Were you on your way to present it to a literary agent in the city?

MARILYN. An agent? No. I'm not ready for something like that yet.

ARTHUR. *(Places a room key on counter.)* If you're looking for a second opinion, I'd love to read it for you. I'm certainly no critic, but I have done my fair share of reading over the years.

MARILYN. Thank you, but I'm kind of picky about who reads my work this early. Besides, no one will be able to read it now until I get it reorganized. *(Goes to take the room key.)* I better get started. It's gonna be a long night.

ARTHUR. Not necessarily. There's a writer's desk in one of the rooms. Last I checked it was filled to the brim with supplies. It would help with organizing all those papers.

MARILYN. That would be great. Thank you. *(Arthur takes back the key and replaces it with another. As he does so, Tom pulls out the money he previously stole from Marilyn's purse and stares at it in contemplation.)*

ARTHUR. Just make sure you stay hydrated while you work.

MARILYN. I will. Have a good night. *(Tom tosses the money onto the couch. He then sets down his trunk and picks up the money as if finding it for the first time. He crosses to Marilyn.)*

TOM. Marilyn! I found this on the couch. I think it's yours.

MARILYN. It is. After that bus ticket, it was all I had left. Thank you. You're a lifesaver. *(She takes the money and exits out the hallway door. Tom drags his trunk over to the counter. He signs in.)*

ARTHUR. That was quite chivalrous of you. *(Reads the name.)* Tom Gav …

TOM. *(Grabs notebook.)* Whoops. Sorry. *(He crosses out last name and rewrites it.)*

ARTHUR. *(Turns the notebook around and reads.)* Ah I see. Tom Garrison. *(Hands him a key and gestures to the trunk.)* You need any help with that?

TOM. I'll be fine. I almost forgot … *(Reaches into pocket and pulls out the pen.)* Borrowed this earlier. Wanted to give it back. *(He places it on the counter.)*

ARTHUR. *(Smiles.)* Get some rest, Tommy. You could use it. *(Tom takes the key and trunk and exits out the hallway door. After a moment, Arthur takes the pen and flips a nearby light switch. The lights dim except for those above the coffee table and the snake cage. He crosses to the snake cage. Angry hisses are heard from within until he waves a hand through the air. He then reaches in and pulls out a snake.)* Interesting group, aren't they? Especially that Tom Gav … excuse me, Tom Garrison. *(The snake angrily hisses.)* Now, Joey, an attitude like that isn't gonna help you. *(The Upstage Right elevator doors open, and The Stranger enters. She wears a white dress. The doors close behind her. Arthur becomes immediately aware of her presence and gives his snake parting words.)* You play nicely now. *(Tosses snake back into cage and addresses The Stranger.)* So, what exactly were you doing out there this evening?

THE STRANGER. I wanted to see what you did with the place, Arthur Nelligan. I see you're back to using that alias.

ARTHUR. And what alias, may I ask, are you using these days?

THE STRANGER. I haven't decided yet. Guess it depends on how things go.

ARTHUR. Until then, how's about a drink? *(Pulls out a deck of playing cards from his pocket.)* And another round of our favorite game? *(He crosses to the coffee table and sits. The Stranger picks up a bottle of white wine from the bar cart and a glass. She sets them both down on the coffee table.)*

THE STRANGER. What will you have?

ARTHUR. *(Shuffles deck.)* Second bottle on the left. First Row. *(The Stranger pulls out the corresponding bottle.)*

THE STRANGER. *(Reads label.)* Kentucky Bourbon. *(Picks up shot glass.)* Why am I not surprised? *(She sets down the bourbon and shot glass and sits across from Arthur. They pour their drinks into their respective glasses. Arthur hands her half the deck. They begin to play a game of war with the cards.)*

ARTHUR. Speaking of surprises, I'm a little taken aback he decided to send you. Surely, he has more experienced candidates. More loyal candidates.

THE STRANGER. We discussed it and he feels that I, and I alone, should be the one to take this particular group of guests from you.

ARTHUR. Glad to see he hasn't lost his sense of humor.

THE STRANGER. Do you really think you'll get them all? Even the girl?

ARTHUR. Especially the girl. Believe me, I've got plenty in store for her. Same for the other two, bless their hearts.

THE STRANGER. You think that by having your name on that plaque out front you have some kind of power over me? You don't. I've got plenty in store for them too.

ARTHUR. I'm glad to hear it. How's about we make things interesting then. What do you say to a little wager?

THE STRANGER. Not a chance. I may be new to this place, but I'm not new to you or your ways. Besides, weren't little wagers what got you stuck here in the first place?

ARTHUR. Indeed they were. Apparently, some of your colleagues were a bit savvier than I realized.

THE STRANGER. Then why are you so eager to bet again?

ARTHUR. Because I like a challenge, and I know you like a challenge too. I also know we're both eager to teach one another a lesson. This would give us that opportunity.

THE STRANGER. And what would this lesson be?

ARTHUR. See! I knew you'd be interested!

THE STRANGER. I haven't agreed to anything yet. I merely asked a question.

ARTHUR. And I have an answer. The bet is this: if you win, you become the next proprietor. Which means from now on you'll have the advantage within these walls. But that's not all. If you win, I'll also add another life sentence to this. *(He picks up a leg to his pants to reveal a house arrest ankle bracelet.)*

THE STRANGER. I become the proprietor and you get another life sentence? *(Considers.)* And what happens if you win?

ARTHUR. I walk out that front door.

THE STRANGER. I figured that suit and tie weren't on the coat rack just for show. I knew you were bold, but I never knew you were delusional.

ARTHUR. You haven't heard the best part yet. To win, you only need to get one of 'em. *(The Stranger freezes halfway through placing down a card.)*

THE STRANGER. What did you say?

ARTHUR. My, my, my. Look who has hearing problems

all of a sudden. You heard me. You get one, doesn't matter which, and I will give you everything I promised. It's all explained in this document. *(He pulls out a document from beneath the coffee table. The Stranger takes it and begins to read.)* Like you, I too was hoping our paths would cross again. I'm just glad they crossed here and now. *(Puts pen on coffee table.)* Well? What're your thoughts?

THE STRANGER. I think … you've gotten rather sloppy with your penmanship. *(Gestures to bottom of document.)* There's a smudge near the last line.

ARTHUR. Anything else?

THE STRANGER. *(Reads it over.)* I don't know. I'm still looking for the "catch."

ARTHUR. I'm afraid there isn't one. Little tricks don't interest me much anymore. What does interest me is discovering where your loyalties lie. After all this time, I'm genuinely curious to see if you're meant to be with him. And deep down, I think you're curious to find out too. All you need to do is get one of them. That's one out of three. Thirty three percent. Surely, he thinks you're capable of getting a measly thirty three percent.

THE STRANGER. I hope you've been comfortable here, Arthur. Because after I'm done with you, you're going to be stuck in this place a little while longer. *(She picks up the pen and signs the document.)*

ARTHUR. Now that's the risk-taker I remember. My turn. *(He takes the pen and signs his portion. The Stranger notices they each have the same number of cards on the table.)*

THE STRANGER. Doesn't look like there's going to be a winner. At least not tonight anyway. *(Arthur pulls out a pocket watch and examines its surface.)*

ARTHUR. Six minutes past midnight. It is now the twenty-second of December. We've officially begun.

THE STRANGER. *(Raises her glass.)* How's about a toast, then? *(Arthur raises his shot glass.)* To the next three days. May the strong rise.

ARTHUR. And may the weak fall. *(They clang glasses and drink. The lights go down.)*

 End of scene.

ACT ONE
Scene 2

The lounge of the Nelligan Motel.

The next morning. December 22nd.

An instrumental Christmas song plays on the radio. A glass of orange juice rests on the coffee table. Gretchen sits on the couch wearing a fake ruby necklace. She finishes the last forkful of her breakfast and sets down her plate. She then reaches into her purse and pulls out a bottle of diet pills. She unscrews the top, takes a pill, and swallows it. After a moment, she takes out another pill and greedily swallows it. She gulps down some orange juice and puts the bottle back in her purse. The hallway door opens, and Tom enters with a mug of coffee.

TOM. Isn't it a little early for tunes?

GRETCHEN. I'm waiting for a weather report. I was hoping to catch one on the news, but the TV in my room has awful reception. *(Tom crosses to the front door and opens it. He stares out into the raging blizzard.)*

TOM. TV in my room has got shit reception too. Anyway, I doubt the report's gonna be good. Not by the look of things. *(Marilyn enters through the hallway door.)*

MARILYN. Good morning.

TOM. *(Closes front door.)* Morning, Marilyn.

GRETCHEN. How're you feeling?

MARILYN. Got a bit of a headache but other than that, I'm okay. *(She takes a seat in one of the chairs, while Tom takes a seat in the other. She notices Gretchen's necklace.)* That's a beautiful necklace. I love the ruby. *(Tom picks up an apple from the fruit bowl and perks up at the mention of the ruby.)*

GRETCHEN. Thank you, but it's not real.

MARILYN. Really? I never would've known. Reminds me of the necklace that heiress on all those magazine covers wears.

GRETCHEN. Evelyn Adamson?

MARILYN. That's it. You know, she got robbed recently.

GRETCHEN. I heard. A pair of robbers broke into her mansion a couple of nights ago. She wasn't home, but her boyfriend was, and he shot one of them. Last I heard the robber who got shot was on life support.

MARILYN. He was on life support. News station they had on at the bus station said they took him off it. *(Tom drops the apple. Gretchen and Marilyn stare.)*

TOM. Sorry. *(He takes his mug and attempts to drink from it. Before either of the women can comment, the song on the radio fades, and the voice on the radio picks up.)*

VOICE ON THE RADIO (V.O). And now for the latest weather report … *(Gretchen and Marilyn rise and cross to the radio. Tom remains seated. Arthur enters through the hallway door. He uses his walker and carries a newspaper.)* The winter storm outside of Pittsburg, which has ravaged the area since yesterday evening, is expected to continue throughout the day, generating at least another foot of snow. The Governor's State of Emergency will remain in effect until further notice. *(Gretchen shuts off the radio.)*

GRETCHEN. I cannot believe this. Another foot of snow?

MARILYN. Hello, Mr. Nelligan.

ARTHUR. Hello Marilyn. Gretchen. Tom. I trust you all slept well.

GRETCHEN. I just wish we woke up to better news.

ARTHUR. I know how hard this must be for y'all especially with the holiday right around the corner. That's why I won't be charging any of you for tonight.

GRETCHEN. Thank you. That's very kind.

MARILYN. Will we be able to keep the same rooms?

ARTHUR. I don't see why not. Unless you wish to be moved.

MARILYN. Not at all. I loved the writer's desk. Speaking of which, there's something I'd like to show you. Be right back. *(She exits out the hallway door.)*

GRETCHEN. I really wish the phone lines were working. My sister-in-law must be so worried about me.

ARTHUR. Is this Chuck's sister, we're talking about?

GRETCHEN. Yes. This'll be my first Christmas with her since he died.

ARTHUR. I'm afraid the phone lines are gonna be down for a few more days. At least, that's what the newspaper said.

GRETCHEN. Newspaper? *(Arthur nods and hands her the newspaper. Gretchen examines it.)* This is today's. How on earth were you able to get this?

ARTHUR. It was the strangest thing. Found it on the front stoop when I woke up this morning. I tell ya, it's remarkable.

GRETCHEN. Unfortunately, the state of it is anything but. *(Looks to first page.)* The front page is missing.

ARTHUR. Is it? Huh. Hopefully it'll turn up soon. *(Marilyn reenters. She carries a manuscript of bound papers. She hands Arthur the manuscript.)*

MARILYN. Took me awhile, but I was finally able to get it in order.

ARTHUR. *(Reads title page.)* The Adventures of Ariadne Longtail by Marilyn Morris. Is this your novel?

MARILYN. It is. You're welcome to read it. As long as you finish it before it's time for us to leave. It's my only copy.

ARTHUR. Don't worry. When it comes to walking, I'm slower than a tortoise, but when it comes to reading, I'm still faster than a Jackrabbit. *(Gretchen sets down the newspaper and examines the manuscript.)*

GRETCHEN. *(Flips through manuscript.)* Did you write all of this by hand?

MARILYN. I did. On notepad paper, scrap paper, even a couple napkins. Whatever I had on me.

GRETCHEN. *(Reads tops of notepad pages.)* Notepad paper from the Bagley Motel. The Brown Motel. *(Turns page.)* The Goodman Motel. The Sutherland Hotel … *That's* in Los Angeles, isn't it?

MARILYN. It is.

GRETCHEN. *(Pages through novel.)* My, you've certainly stayed at a lot of motels and hotels.

ARTHUR. That just means she likes to travel. Hopefully you'll all get back to traveling soon.

GRETCHEN. If this infernal blizzard lets up.

ARTHUR. Say some extra prayers that it lets up sooner rather than later. Marilyn can help you there.

MARILYN. Help with what?

ARTHUR. With some prayers. You know. Getting down on your knees, placing your hands together, asking someone for a favor.

MARILYN. What makes you think I pray?

ARTHUR. I heard you mention last night that your father

was a minister. I assumed…

MARILYN. *(Rubs head.)* I haven't prayed since I was a kid.

ARTHUR. My, my, my. I always thought the whole, "rebellious minister's daughter" was just a stereotype in poorly written TV shows. *(Playful.)* Tell me, how does Daddy feel about this?

MARILYN. Daddy hasn't felt anything in years. *(Rubs head some more.)* He died when I was eight.

ARTHUR. Oh, Marilyn. Please forgive me. I had no idea. *(He touches her arm. She winces and touches her head again.)* Something wrong?

MARILYN. My headache's getting bad again. I think I'll head back to my room. Maybe lie down for a bit. *(She proceeds to the hallway door. Arthur calls out to her.)*

ARTHUR. Marilyn… *(Smiles)* Ever have one of those days you wish you could start over?

MARILYN. *(Smiles.)* Too many to count.

ARTHUR. *(Gestures to the manuscript.)* I'll be sure to read this with the upmost care.

MARILYN. Thank you, Mr. Nelligan. I'll see you later. *(She exits out the hallway door.)*

GRETCHEN. I think I'll follow her lead. Seeing how we're going to be here longer; I might as well unpack some more.

ARTHUR. Don't lose track of time. Wouldn't want you to miss lunch.

GRETCHEN. You're making us lunch too?

ARTHUR. Of course. Y'all are still my guests, aren't ya?

GRETCHEN. Yes, but the breakfast you made me was more than enough.

ARTHUR. Oh, come now. It was only French toast.

GRETCHEN. Stuffed with some of the most mouth-watering apples I've ever tasted. *(Jokingly.)* Need I remind you, I'm trying to lose weight, not gain it?

ARTHUR. It's the holidays. You're supposed to indulge. But if you are feeling guilty, you could always take one of those little diet helpers you were telling me about. That is, if you haven't taken any today yet.

GRETCHEN. *(Contemplates.)* No. No, I haven't taken any today. *(She pulls the pill bottle out of her purse and unscrews the top. She pops another pill into her mouth and smiles.)*

ARTHUR. *(Points to her necklace.)* I do declare, that is a stunning piece of jewelry. Gift from Chuck, I take it?

GRETCHEN. No, this was from someone else. *(Twiddles necklace.)* I'll see you at lunch. *(She exits. Arthur notices Tom still sitting.)*

ARTHUR. Tommy! I forgot you were still sitting there.

TOM. Sorry. I guess I've been a little quiet.

ARTHUR. Saying you've been a little quiet, is like saying Cain was a little tense when he killed Abel. I do hope everything is all right.

TOM. I've had a lot on my mind lately. I think I'm gonna sit out here for a bit if that's okay.

ARTHUR. Take as much time as you like. *(Gestures to newspaper.)* Feel free to do some reading. I know the news can be a drag, but the funny pages are always good for a laugh.

TOM. Thanks.

ARTHUR. You're welcome, Tommy.

TOM. Please don't call me, Tommy. My grandfather would call me that all the time.

ARTHUR. Is this the same grandfather you lived with? The one who'd send you into town to get apples?

TOM. Yeah. That's the one. *(He examines Arthur's eyes*

peering down at him.) You know, Mr. Nelligan, this is gonna sound crazy, but you remind me of him a bit. You have his eyes.

ARTHUR. I'll take that as a compliment. And please, call me, Arthur. *(He crosses to the hallway door with his walker. Tom picks up the newspaper.)*

TOM. I still can't believe a paperboy made a delivery today.

ARTHUR. Yes, I reckon a person would have to be very foolish to venture out into a storm like this. Or very desperate. *(He exits out the hallway door. Tom looks down at the page before him and becomes alarmed by what he sees. Frantic, he pages through the paper and stops on an article. He reads it to himself and becomes visibly troubled. He rips out the article, folds it up, and puts it in his pocket, unaware the Upstage Right elevator doors are opening. The Stranger enters. The elevator doors close behind her. The lights flicker.)*

TOM. Hey, Mr. Nelligan? Arthur? *(The lights stop flickering. Tom notices The Stranger and becomes startled. He rises.)* What the …?!

THE STRANGER. My time within these walls is short, Tom, so listen to me carefully.

TOM. How do you know my name?

THE STRANGER. Sam asked me to warn you.

TOM. Sam?

THE STRANGER. It's not too late. It's not too late to be true to yourself. *(Takes his hands.)* You're not your brother. No matter how much you try to convince yourself otherwise.

TOM. *(Pushes her hands away.)* When did you talk to Sam?

THE STRANGER. Right before I came here.

TOM. *(Grabs a hold of her.)* That's impossible. You hear me? That's impossible!

THE STRANGER. Stay clear of anything that slithers. That's what Sam used to tell you whenever you'd go on walks together through the swamp. And that's what I'm telling you now. If you want to be the person Sam knew you to be, you'll stay clear. You'll stay clear no matter what. *(The lights flicker until they BLACKOUT. After a few seconds, the lights come back up again. Tom remains standing in place with his hands in the same position, but The Stranger is no longer in his grasp. The front door has been left ajar and the howl of the wind is heard outside. Tom reaches into the back of his pants and pulls out a gun. With the gun raised in his hand, he cautiously approaches the front door and opens it. He stares outside where the blizzard continues to rage. After a moment, he lowers the gun and closes the door. The radio turns on by itself, causing him to raise the gun once more.)*

VOICE ON THE RADIO (V.O.) …and now for a breaking update on the blizzard outside of Pittsburgh. Our weather desk has confirmed the storm will end around midnight tonight. We repeat the winter storm will end around midnight tonight. Cleanup efforts on the roads leading into the city will begin immediately. *(The voice fizzles away and the radio shuts off. Tom hides the gun in the back of his pants once more. He looks around the lounge for any sign of The Stranger, only to focus on the snake cage. The sound of faint hissing and the sound of snakes flopping about are heard. Tom listens for a moment before he snaps out of his trance and exits out the hallway door.)*

End of scene

ACT ONE
Scene 3

The lounge of the Nelligan Motel.

A few hours later. Night.

The lounge is dimly lit. Through the darkness, Tom enters from the hallway, dragging his trunk. He puts on his winter coat at the coat rack, crosses to the front door, and opens it to reveal a calm and serene night. He takes a deep breath and steps outside with the trunk. As he disappears, the blizzard suddenly picks up without warning. He then staggers back inside with the trunk, defeated and gasping for air. Outside, the wind howls. Tom rushes to the door and closes it shut.

TOM. What the …!? *(Throws coat on floor.)* Son of a bitch. *(The lights go up to reveal Arthur sitting in the armchair and reading a newspaper. A shot glass and the bourbon bottle rest on the stand beside him.)*

ARTHUR. I'm afraid foul language isn't going to help your situation.

TOM. Arthur! What are you doing up?

ARTHUR. Couldn't sleep, so I decided to do some late-night reading. *(Looks at newspaper.)* Huh. There seems to be an article missing. I wonder if it's the same article I have here in my pocket. *(He reaches into his pocket and pulls out a folded newspaper page. It is the exact same page Tom withdrew and folded earlier. Arthur unfolds it and holds it to the newspaper.)* What do ya know? Like finding a missing puzzle piece.

TOM. *(Checks his own pocket.)* How … how did you get that?!

ARTHUR. Let's just say, I learned from the best. *(Reads newspaper article.)* "Brothers Joseph and Thomas Gavin, who have been identified as the culprits in a string of robberies, robbed the estate of millionaire heiress, Evelyn Adamson, earlier this week. During the getaway, Joseph Gavin was shot and killed by Ms. Adamson's boyfriend, who was housesitting the property. Thomas Gavin, however, remains at large and is believed to be heading towards the Pittsburgh area. He is expected to be armed, dangerous, and in possession of several of Miss Adamson's stolen items …" Hmmm, I gotta say, the picture they printed of this Tom Gavin looks a lot like you, Tom Garrison.

TOM. Enough. What do you want?

ARTHUR. For right now, I just want to talk. I mean, it's not every day I get to play host to someone like yourself. Why, you and your brother had your hands in more safes this past month than most bank managers do in a year! How many mansions did you two hit? *(No response.)* Come on, man. You really think I'm gonna rat you out when things are starting to get interesting? How many mansions?

TOM. About a dozen. We saved Evelyn's for last because we heard she was going to be out of the country.

ARTHUR. Sounded like a solid strategy. It's just a shame you didn't know her gun-toting boy-toy would be there. I can understand him wanting to protect his woman's property, but to shoot your brother in the back like that …

TOM. Wait. How do you know where Joseph was shot? That wasn't in the paper.

ARTHUR. Just a guess. You should know by now I'm full

of guesses. *(Nods to trunk.)* Take that trunk for instance. I'm willing to guess it was once filled to the brim with Evelyn's belongings.

TOM. Once filled? *(He hurries to the trunk. Arthur rises with his walker. Tom opens the trunk and lays it on its side. It is completely empty.)* What did you do with it? What did you do with everything that was in here? *(He reaches into the backend of his pants and pulls out the gun. He aims the gun at Arthur.)*

ARTHUR. I was wondering when that would be making an appearance!

TOM. *(Nervous.)* Where's the stuff you took!? Don't make me shoot you.

ARTHUR. Come on, Tom. Look at yourself. You're sweaty. You're nervous. You're not a killer. Why, you look more like an awkward high school kid who's about to lose his virginity to the hot cheerleader ... or in your case, the hot quarterback.

TOM. What did you just say to me?

ARTHUR. Nothing more than your grandfather said a hundred times. Especially after he took you and Joseph to that brothel ... *(He clears his throat. His voice drastically changes by the time he speaks. He mimics a voice that could resemble Tom's grandfather.)* What's the matter with you, Tommy?! I finally arrange for you to get a girl, and all you do is talk with her?! I should've known what you were when you started going on walks through the swamp with that boy from school! *(Moves closer.)* This is all your mother's doing. I warned my son about having kids with a dumb twat like her, but he wouldn't listen. Then he dies, she dies, and I get stuck with you!

TOM. YOU SON OF A BITCH! *(He strikes Arthur with the back of the gun. Arthur tumbles to the floor with his walker. He lays on the floor withering in pain.)*

ARTHUR. *(Back to his normal speaking voice.)* Why'd you do that?! Why!?

TOM. Arthur? *(Leans over to help.)* Shit. I'm sorry. For a second, I thought you were my … *(Without warning, Arthur reaches up and yanks the gun out of his hand. He points the gun at Tom.)*

ARTHUR. *(Laughs.)* Oh, Tom. If you're gonna climb into the lion's den, you can't let your guard down when you finally face the lion. *(He slithers over to the armchair and retakes his seat. He then examines the gun.)* Over the years, I've seen so many people get creative with a gun like this. I've seen "scrambled eggs" to the left … *(Puts the gun to his left temple.)* … and I've seen "scrambled eggs," to the right. *(Puts the gun to his right temple.)* I've also seen what I like to call "the chin scratcher." *(Puts the gun below his chin.)* You wouldn't believe how far the brains fly out when you fire a bullet into them like that. *(Leans back in the armchair with the gun below his chin.)* What do ya think? You think my brains would hit the back wall, or do you think they'd hit the snake cage?

TOM. Stop it! STOP IT! Put the gun down and stop it!

ARTHUR. Nah, if I was gonna end it all, I'd go with the "heartbreaker." *(Aims gun over his heart.)* After all, that's how Sam took his life, wasn't it? Right after his mom overdosed and right after your grandfather forced you to end things with him. *(Cocks gun.)* You know, I've always wondered what was worse. A broken heart, or a dead one. Let's find out.

TOM. Arthur, no. NO! *(Arthur pulls the trigger only for the gun to emit a clicking sound.)*

ARTHUR. *(Laughs.)* Tommy, Tommy, Tommy. I'm disappointed. You should know by now, that a gun without bullets is truly useless! *(He drops the gun into the garbage can. Tom approaches and pulls out the gun. He examines it.)*

TOM. I don't understand. I loaded this. I know because I fired off a warning shot at Evelyn's place. I made sure I ... *(He pulls the trigger and the gun fires. He drops it on the floor.)* SHIT! *(Arthur reaches up his sleeve and pulls out a large ruby necklace. Tom notices.)* What is that? Is that ...?

ARTHUR. You know what it is. Her initials are inscribed on the back and everything. *(Gestures to inscription.)* E. A. Evelyn Adamson.

TOM. But that was in Joseph's hand when he got shot. He had one hand on the car door and the other on that. It was still in his hand when I drove away.

ARTHUR. If you don't believe me, come and see for yourself. *(Tom cautiously approaches. He examines the necklace.)*

TOM. It is her necklace. How did you get it?!

ARTHUR. I could tell you. Or I could just give it to you.

TOM. What?

ARTHUR. It's what you want, isn't it? It's what you've wanted ever since you were a little boy. Ever since you saw the news story on Evelyn Adamson and her jewelry. You prayed for a necklace like this, because you knew it would pay for your mother's treatments. And your prayers fell on deaf ears. You prayed for it after you and Joseph went to live with your grandfather. You knew that with a necklace like this, you and Sam would be rich enough to move away and never see anyone like your grandfather again. And your prayers fell on deaf ears. After Sam killed himself, you decided it was time to start answering your own prayers. So, you joined your brother who helped you find ways to obtain the finer things in life. All those robberies, all those wonderful things he helped you acquire. It was addictive, wasn't it?

TOM. It was. Until he got shot.

ARTHUR. Over this. *(Gestures to necklace.)* The great Joseph Gavin. Apple of your grandfather's eye, brought down by the one thing you always wanted; the one thing that is now finally within your reach. Tell me, Tom, what exactly were you gonna do once you left this place? Turn yourself in? Pray for forgiveness?

TOM. I don't know exactly. In his suicide note, Sam told me to be true to myself. *(Stares at necklace.)* I guess I'm still trying to figure out who I really am.

ARTHUR. *(Mimics a voice that could resemble Tom's grandfather.)* I'll tell ya who you really are. A disgrace. A pathetic disgrace who can't do anything right!

TOM. Stop it. Stop it …

ARTHUR. *(Mimics a voice that could resemble Tom's grandfather.)* Even when you was a kid, you'd be messing everything up. When I'd send you and your brother into town, Joey would bring me back the fresh apples. You'd bring me back the rotten ones. Joey would pickpocket the rich tourists and come back with hundred dollar bills. You'd pickpocket the poor freaks and come back with chump change.

TOM. Shut up. SHUT UP!

ARTHUR. *(Mimics a voice that could resemble Tom's grandfather.)* Why can't you be like Joey, Tommy? For once in your life, why can't you be like your brother? *(Leans towards him.)* Do I have to beat it out of ya like I did after I caught you with that boy? Because I will. I will keep beating it out of ya until you can look me in the eye like a real man! *(Tom picks up the gun and grabs a hold of Arthur.)*

TOM. You son of a bitch! YOU SON OF A BITCH! *(Puts gun to Arthur's temple.)* Give it to me. GIVE IT TO ME OR

YOU'RE DEAD! *(Arthur chuckles and clears his throat. His voice returns to normal.)*

ARTHUR. That a boy, Tommy. That a boy! *(He drops the necklace into Tom's open hand. The Upstage Left elevator doors open by themselves.)* All the items from your trunk are down in the basement. Go on. Treat yourself. You've earned it. *(He pours himself a shot of bourbon. Tom enters the elevator.)*

TOM. *(Searches the walls.)* Where are all the buttons? *(Examines necklace as if for first time.)* Wait a minute. This … this isn't the necklace. This is a toy. This is some cheap mean … meaning … less t … t… toy … *(Clutches his stomach.)* Oh … God! What's happening? WHAT'SSS HAPPENING TO ME!? *(He screams in pain and drops the necklace and the gun. He collapses to the elevator floor, clutching his stomach.)* Arthur, help! HELP ME, PLEASE! *(Arthur toasts the shot glass.)*

ARTHUR. "I will bring on them a disaster they cannot escape. Although they cry out to me, I will not listen to them."

TOM. *(Convulsing violently.)* Mama! MAMA! HELP ME, MAMA! *(The lights flash red and flicker as the elevator doors begin to close. By the time the doors fully close and stifle the last of Tom's screams, Arthur downs his shot of bourbon. The lights continue to flicker until they BLACKOUT. After a few seconds, the lights come back up again. Arthur stares at his empty shot glass with complete satisfaction.)*

ARTHUR. Now that's the good stuff. *(The hallway door opens, and Marilyn enters. She wears a nightgown.)* Oh, good evening, Marilyn! What can I do for you?

MARILYN. I just came to grab a bottle of water from the bar cart.

ARTHUR. Of course, help yourself.

MARILYN. Are you alone right now?

ARTHUR. As far as I know. Why?

MARILYN. I thought I heard you talking to someone.

ARTHUR. You must've heard the radio. I was listening to it a few minutes ago but I shut it off. I hope it didn't wake you.

MARILYN. No, I woke up from cramps. I got another headache too. *(Searches bar cart.)* I don't see any water bottles. I guess I'll take a glass and fill it up with some tap water from the bathroom.

ARTHUR. No offense, Marilyn, but it doesn't seem like water is doing much for all those headaches and cramps you've been getting. *(Gestures to bar cart.)* How's about you try a little something different?

MARILYN. I don't drink.

ARTHUR. The drink I was referring to is non-alcoholic. It should be between the bottles of red and white wine. *(Marilyn pulls out a thermos from the back row. She opens it and looks inside.)*

MARILYN. Looks like apple juice. *(Smells.)* Smells like apple juice.

ARTHUR. Come sit by me and try it. *(Marilyn grabs a chair and places it beside the armchair.)*

MARILYN. *(Takes a sip.)* That's good. *(Takes another sip.)* That's really good.

ARTHUR. Now that you're here, would you mind doing me a favor? I was bringing up some laundry from the basement, and I think I dropped some things in the elevator. Could you check? *(She sets down the drink and rises. She approaches the wall by the elevators and presses a button. The Upstage Left elevator doors open. Tom's clothes lie in a heap on the floor. The gun and fake necklace are gone, and Tom is nowhere to be seen. Marilyn scoops up the clothes.)*

MARILYN. Yeah, you dropped some stuff. Where do you want it?

ARTHUR. *(Gestures to floor.)* Here's fine. *(She dumps the clothes on the floor.)* Better get them in order.

MARILYN. I got it. *(Starts to untangle the clothes.)* These must've just come out of the dryer. They're still warm. *(A hiss comes from within the pile of clothes. Marilyn lifts a fold and recoils in horror as she screams.)* SNAKE! SNAKE! *(Arthur moves the shirt aside to reveal a snake.)*

ARTHUR. My, my, my. What're you doing in there?

MARILYN. GET IT AWAY FROM ME! GET IT AWAY FROM ME! *(Arthur takes the snake and dumps it into the garbage can.)*

ARTHUR. That'll hold him. He must've gotten into the laundry basket somehow. I do apologize. *(Marilyn is still trembling in fear. Arthur picks up the thermos and offers it to her.)* Here, drink some more. It'll help with the shock. Go on. *(Marilyn takes the thermos and drinks. As she does so, Arthur scoops up the shirt, pants, and socks and puts them into the garbage can.)*

MARILYN. My father was bitten by a snake.

ARTHUR. I beg your pardon.

MARILYN. When I was eight, he agreed to serve as a missionary pastor out in India, and my mother and I went to live with him. One day, the two of us were on a walk and were about ready to turn back to our village, when I saw a flower near some high grass. I had gotten into a huge fight with my mother earlier that morning, and I figured I could give it to her when I apologized. I let go of my father's hand and ran for the flower and was about to pick it when I saw it. Right by my feet, and crawling through the grass, was a cobra. It lunged for me, but my father managed to push me out of the way. By the time I realized what had happened, the snake had already sunk its fangs into his leg. I ran back the way we came, screaming so much, that by the time I finally got back to the village, I could barely talk. My mother found some locals to help us, and I led them to where he was, all the while, saying every prayer I could think of. By the time we reached him, he could barely move. The nurse at the hospital later told us the venom from the cobra attacks the nerves on the muscles and eventually paralyzes them. She also explained in some instances, the

venom can cause cardiac arrest. Despite what she told us, I prayed, and I prayed, right until the moment the doctor came out and told us the news. Do you know what the odds were of that cobra being there at that moment, biting my father, and the bite being so severe it caused cardiac arrest? I'll tell you. He literally had a better chance of winning the lottery and getting struck by lightning on the same day. When my mother and I got back to the states, members of the church would come up to us and say things like, "everything happens for a reason," and that "we would see him again someday." But the older I got, the more I realized there was no purpose in what happened. It's as if what happened had happened out of spite.

ARTHUR. That was the last time you prayed, wasn't it? The afternoon your father died.

MARILYN. *(Nods.)* If a higher being wouldn't answer prayers to save a man like him, why would he answer prayers to save any of us? *(Takes a long sip from thermos.)* You know, I've never tasted apple juice like this before.

ARTHUR. Want to know a secret? I take frozen apple juice and I add extra sugar. A lot of extra sugar. Don't tell anybody though. Everybody who tries it, thinks it's homemade.

MARILYN. *(Smiles.)* Your secret's safe with me.

ARTHUR. *(Jokingly.)* I wouldn't be too sure about that. If

I recall, Kristi said something similar to Ariadne Longtail down in the grotto right before she betrayed her.

MARILYN. You're that far into my book already?

ARTHUR. I told you I read fast. Never did I think I'd be on the edge of my seat reading a fantasy book about mermaids and magic tridents, but here I am. I can't wait to read the rest of it. You have a wonderful imagination.

MARILYN. Growing up, I'd always play make believe, and dream up stories with my dad. A lot of the stories we told each other actually ended up in this book.

ARTHUR. He sounds like he was a remarkable man. I'm sure he'd be very proud of the woman you've become. *(Marilyn gives a weak smile and takes another sip of her drink. She stares at it.)* Is something wrong? I didn't make it too sweet, did I?

MARILYN. No, it's fine. It's just … my headache and cramps feel better.

ARTHUR. Maybe you just needed to sit down and talk about your problems. Like I always say, "most of the time, your problems don't seem all that bad when you're sitting down." *(Marilyn looks into Arthur's eyes.)*

MARILYN. You know, you remind me of my father. You have his eyes.

ARTHUR. *(Smiles.)* I'll take that as a compliment.

MARILYN. You should. It was meant as one. I think I'll head back to bed now. When I checked the clock on my dresser it was ten minutes to midnight and that was about ten minutes ago. I'll see you in the morning. *(She rises with the thermos and crosses to the hallway door.)*

ARTHUR. Do you believe you'll get to see him again, Marilyn?

MARILYN. Who?

ARTHUR. Your father. *(Marilyn ponders for a moment.)*

MARILYN. No. As morbid as it sounds, I believe when we die, we simply fade away into nothing.

ARTHUR. If that's true, then I believe we all need to live our lives to the fullest. That means seizing every opportunity that presents itself and letting go of all regrets. *(He lets Marilyn take that in for a moment.)* Get some sleep, sweetheart. Rest that wonderful imagination.

MARILYN. Goodnight, Mr. Nelligan.

ARTHUR. Please. Call me, Arthur.

MARILYN. *(Smiles.)* Okay. Goodnight, Arthur. *(She exits out the hallway door. Arthur pulls out the snake from the wastebasket. The snake angrily hisses.)*

ARTHUR. Like I told you before, Tommy, foul language isn't going to help your situation. Now, I understand this is a big adjustment for you. It was for all the others, and I'm sure it will be for the rest of our current guests as well. But in the end, you will all come to accept it. After all, it's not like you have a choice. *(He rises and grabs a hold of the walker, only to realize he no longer needs it. With a pair of wobbly legs, he crosses to the snake cage.)* "Stand upright on your feet. And he leaped up and began to walk." *(He tosses the snake into the cage, causing all the other snakes within to hiss in horror. He then cackles in triumph.)*

END OF ACT I

ACT TWO
Scene 1

The lounge of the Nelligan Motel.

The next morning. December 23rd.

Gretchen sits on the couch. She holds a plate on her lap and eats the last forkful of her breakfast. A glass of orange juice rests on the coffee table and her purse rests beside her. She sets down the plate. As she does so, she listens to the radio. The Voice on the Radio is heard.

VOICE ON THE RADIO (V.O.). Despite record snowfall, sanitation workers remain confident all major roads will be cleared in time for holiday travel to resume tomorrow. And now back to some instrumental classics. *(Soft instrumental ballet music begins to play. Gretchen immediately perks up.)*

GRETCHEN. Oh my … *(After making sure she is alone, she rises, closes her eyes, and begins to twirl to the rhythm of the music. She dances before the radio, lost in her own little world, until she touches her body. Disappointed, she opens her eyes, and looks down in disgust. She reaches into her purse and pulls out the bottle of diet pills. She unscrews the top and pours some pills into her hand. She stares at the pills in contemplation until the sound of approaching footsteps is heard. She then shoves the pills into her mouth and throws the bottle back into her purse. She shuts off the radio as Marilyn enters.)*

MARILYN. Good morning.

GRETCHEN. Morning. *(Downs her orange juice.)* Sorry, I was just finishing my breakfast. I ate out here so I could hear the weather report. Storm's finally over.

MARILYN. That's great news. You'll have to tell Tom too.

GRETCHEN. I would but he's already gone.

MARILYN. Wait. He … left?

GRETCHEN. According to the registry. I also peeped inside his room on my way out here. It's completely cleared out.

MARILYN. *(Examines notebook.)* Says he checked out at six a.m. He must've left on foot.

GRETCHEN. I knew he was desperate to get out of here. I didn't think he was that desperate.

MARILYN. Me neither. *(Gestures to radio.)* What was the song that was playing when I walked in?

GRETCHEN. It's from a ballet. *(Twiddles necklace.)* In fact, it was the last song I danced to as a ballerina.

MARILYN. Wow. I had no idea. It must mean a lot to you then.

GRETCHEN. More now than ever. *(Looks her over.)* You look … well, Marilyn. I mean, really well.

MARILYN. I feel well. In fact, I feel fantastic.

GRETCHEN. Seems this little detour was what you needed. If you don't mind me asking, where were you originally headed before we all ended up here?

MARILYN. I was on my way to my mother's.

GRETCHEN. Oh dear. She must be worried sick about you.

MARILYN. She actually doesn't know I'm coming. *(Considers.)* We haven't spoken in a very long time.

GRETCHEN. If there's one thing I've learned about overdue reunions, it's that they usually go best with a peace offering. *(She reaches into her purse and pulls out some money.)*

When you get to the city, buy her a nice Christmas present.

MARILYN. What? Gretchen, no, I couldn't possibly take …

GRETCHEN. You're not taking anything. I'm giving it to you.

MARILYN. Still. You barely know me.

GRETCHEN. I know you're someone who's trying to better herself. I find that admirable. Please. Take it. I guarantee, it'll make you and her much happier than it will me. *(Marilyn ponders for a moment before she takes the money. Unbeknownst to either of them, Arthur enters from the Offstage hallway. He looks significantly younger and walks with the assistance of a cane.)*

MARILYN. *(Genuinely moved.)* I don't know what to say. Thank you.

GRETCHEN. It's never too late to do the right thing. Remember that when you see your mother again. *(She becomes aware of Arthur's presence. Marilyn turns and notices him too. Arthur crosses behind the counter and rummages through some drawers.)*

ARTHUR. Don't mind me. I'm just looking for something. Got it. *(He withdraws a hand mirror and sets it on the counter.)*

GRETCHEN. Excuse me, sir. Guests aren't allowed behind the counter. If you want to check in, you'll have to speak with the proprietor. His name is …

MARILYN. Arthur?

GRETCHEN. *(Realizes its him.)* Mr. Nelligan?!

ARTHUR. Morning, Marilyn. Morning, Gretchen.

GRETCHEN. *(Looks him over.)* What on earth happened to you? *(Arthur crosses to the couch. He sits along with Gretchen and Marilyn.)*

ARTHUR. Like I told you earlier, I am expected to make a

full recovery. That confounded walker was only temporary. As you can tell by the cane, I'm still not a hundred percent, but I'm getting there. Slowly but surely. I'm not sure if you ladies noticed, but we are now a trio instead of a quartet. Tommy decided to slither on out of here and try his luck at the nearest town.

MARILYN. Gretchen told me he was gone. It's a shame he left like that. I would've really liked to have said goodbye.

GRETCHEN. Going back to what you said, it's not just the walker, Mr. Nelligan. It's your entire appearance. You look so … so … *(Stares into his eyes.)* Your eyes. They almost remind me of … if you'll excuse me. *(She rises with her glass in hand.)*

MARILYN. I think what Gretchen is trying to say is you look younger. A lot younger.

ARTHUR. Oh, it's just a little makeover. It's not as if someone can magically de-age. Unless of course you're Ariadne Longtail after taking a bath in the fountain of youth.

MARILYN. You finished my novel? What did you think?

ARTHUR. I thought it was masterful. I really hope you'll be dropping it off with a literary agent soon.

MARILYN. I was actually planning on showing it to my mother first.

ARTHUR. Now I understand why you were so protective of it earlier. I already put it back in your satchel for you.

MARILYN. Thanks. I just wish it looked more presentable.

ARTHUR. Well, we might be able to fix that before you go. After all, 'tis the season for miracles, right? Tell me, have you written anything else?

MARILYN. I wrote a play years ago, but …

ARTHUR. You're a playwright too! Just when I think you can't impress me any further, you go on to prove me wrong.

MARILYN. I wouldn't say that just yet. It was produced at this theater outside of Pittsburgh for one weekend and then it closed. The director allowed me to sit backstage on opening night and from what I saw, there were only a dozen people in the audience including a critic who ripped it to shreds. By the time it was over, only one person in the back had the decency to stand and clap because everyone else had fallen asleep.

ARTHUR. All well, at least the theater thought it was good enough to produce. *(Gretchen notices the mirror.)*

MARILYN. I'm not sure if good had anything to do with it. I was living with the director at the time. After the play failed, we both felt like we had something to prove. So we moved from Pittsburgh to Los Angeles and we … *(Gretchen picks up the mirror and gazes into the glass.)*

GRETCHEN. *(Gasps.)* Oh my God. *(Arthur rises and crosses to her. He takes back the mirror.)*

ARTHUR. Please, don't touch that. It's very delicate.

GRETCHEN. I … I saw my reflection in the glass.

ARTHUR. *(Playful.)* Yes. That's how mirrors work.

GRETCHEN. No, I didn't see myself as I am now. I saw myself as I was. Back when I was a ballerina. Let me show you. *(She takes the mirror and gazes into it again only to become disappointed.)* Wait. There must be something wrong with this.

ARTHUR. Gretchen, could I speak with you in private? *(He leads her to the snake cage.)*

GRETCHEN. I know it sounds crazy, but I'm telling you the truth. I know what I saw.

ARTHUR. And did you see this before or after some adult beverages?

GRETCHEN. Please, I haven't had a drink since last night.

ARTHUR. What about those little diet helpers you take?

How many of those have you had this morning?

GRETCHEN. No more than usual.

ARTHUR. And what is the usual number? *(Gretchen gazes into the mirror. The sight brings her back to reality.)* I'm certainly no expert, but I do know if you keep taking enough of those helpers, they'll be helping you to see all sorts of things.

GRETCHEN. *(Hands him back mirror.)* I feel like such a fool. *(Arthur crosses behind the counter and puts the mirror back in the drawer.)*

ARTHUR. Don't feel bad. If anything, you may have given Marilyn some ideas for a future story. *(To Marilyn.)* A magic mirror with the ability to see into the past. I think that would be great in a sequel to Ariadne Longtail.

MARILYN. You think I should write a sequel? Where would I begin?

ARTHUR. I have a couple ideas. I can share them with you after I wash the dishes.

MARILYN. How's about you tell me while we wash the dishes together?

ARTHUR. You've got yourself a deal. *(Marilyn takes the dishes and rises. She crosses to the hallway door and exits. Arthur goes to join her when he observes Gretchen transfixed on the snake cage.)* You all right, Gretchen?

GRETCHEN. The one snake in the back corner keeps looking at me and bumping his head against the glass. If I didn't know better, I'd say he was trying to tell me something.

ARTHUR. Oh, don't mind him. I reckon he's a little antsy because he's new to the group.

GRETCHEN. I'm sorry for my behavior earlier, Mr. Nelligan.

ARTHUR. You have nothing to be sorry for, Gretch. And

please, call me, Arthur. *(He exits. Gretchen remains staring at the snakes. The Upstage Right elevator doors open. The Stranger enters and the elevator doors close behind her. She uses a cane to walk and appears much older. The lights above flicker as she approaches. Gretchen becomes alerted to her presence and spins around.)*

GRETCHEN. *(Surprised.)* Oh my goodness! Who are you?

THE STRANGER. Ted Randall still loves you, Gretchen. Even after all these years, he still loves his butterfly wings.

GRETCHEN. What? How on earth do you know about Ted? Or us?

THE STRANGER. If you choose to embrace the person you were, rather than the person you've become, all will be revealed. *(Places a hand on her shoulder.)* "Though our outer self is wasting away, our inner self is being renewed day by day." *(The lights flicker until they BLACKOUT. After a few seconds, the lights come back up again. The Stranger is gone, and Gretchen stands by herself. A sudden gust of wind pushes the front door inward. Gretchen crosses to the couch, reaches into her purse and pulls out the bottle of diet pills. After staring at the bottle in contemplation, she crosses to the front door and tosses the pills outside. She then closes the front door, scoops up her purse and throws the empty bottle into the trash can. She exits out the hallway door.)*

 End of scene.

ACT TWO
Scene 2

The lounge of the Nelligan Motel.

A few hours later. Night.

The lounge is dimly lit. A figure stands beside the bar cart. Gretchen enters from the hallway. She appears physically ill. She sneaks behind the counter and approaches the drawer where Arthur hid the mirror. She carefully opens the drawer, withdraws the mirror, and flicks on a light switch. The lights go up over the coffee table. Satisfied, she crosses to the couch. As she approaches, Marilyn emerges from beside the bar cart. She holds the thermos.

GRETCHEN. *(Startled.)* Marilyn! *(Hides mirror behind her back.)*

MARILYN. I'm sorry. I didn't mean to scare you. I was just getting some juice Arthur made me before I went to bed. *(She observes Gretchen.)* Are you okay?

GRETCHEN. Yeah. I just couldn't sleep.

MARILYN. Arthur says the phone lines should be working by tomorrow morning, so I'm getting up early to call a taxi. If I don't see you, have a great holiday.

GRETCHEN. You too. Say hello to your mother for me when you see her.

MARILYN. I will. Say hi to your sister-in-law for me too.

And give her my sympathies about Chuck. *(She exits out the hallway door. Gretchen sets the mirror down on the couch, and crosses to the bar cart. She grabs the bottle of brandy and a glass. She carries the bottle and the glass back to the couch and sets them down. She then picks up the mirror, stares into the glass, and becomes instantly overcome with disappointment.)*

GRETCHEN. *(Into mirror.)* Damn it. Goddamn it. *(She sets down the mirror and looks at her stomach in disgust. She pours herself a drink when the lights above BLACKOUT.)* Marilyn? *(Through the darkness, the radio springs to life.)*

VOICE ON THE RADIO (V.O). We have breaking news this evening outside of Pittsburgh. We have received reports that former city mayor, Chuck Hunter, has died following a fall down the stairs in his Pennsylvania home. Hunter was once a favored candidate for governor but a series of health issues forced him to drop out of the race. He is survived by his wife, Gretchen, a former ballerina with the Pittsburgh Ballet…" *(The lights in the room go up to reveal Arthur sitting in the armchair. He now holds the mirror in his hand. A shot glass and bourbon bottle rest on the stand beside him.)*

ARTHUR. *(Into mirror.)* This belonged to a Southern belle.

GRETCHEN. Arthur! *(Notices he has mirror.)* How did you …?

ARTHUR. She was engaged to a Confederate soldier who was wounded during battle and became separated from his platoon. He sought refuge at a nearby home, unaware it belonged to a family of inbred delinquents. They cut off his hands and feet with meat cleavers, and then, while he was still alive, fed him to some rather hungry pigs. When the woman found out what had happened, her raven black hair turned white, and she lost her slim figure. She deteriorated to the point where she was willing to accept death. That was until one day, when a charming stranger arrived at her doorstep and gave her this. *(Gestures to the mirror.)* From that moment on, whenever the woman gazed into the glass, she'd see herself as she once was. Young, beautiful, and planning a future with the man she lost.

GRETCHEN. How does it work?

ARTHUR. I can't say. You see, the stranger who gave it to her was a magician, and magicians never reveal their secrets.

GRETCHEN. I only saw myself young in it once. Every time I've looked at it since, I've only seen myself as I am now. Why didn't you say anything when I told you what I saw this morning? You knew I was telling the truth.

ARTHUR. I didn't want to divulge too much information with Marilyn in the room. Given what the mirror can do, it wouldn't have been wise for someone with an addictive personality like hers to know about it. It'd be like giving a cow too much food. It'll just keep eating and eating until … *(Mimics an exploding sound as he pours a shot of bourbon.)* Of course, you'd know all about such things having grown up on a farm.

GRETCHEN. How did you know where I grew up?

ARTHUR. You mentioned it earlier. I believe you mentioned it after you had an adult beverage mixed with some diet helpers. I can understand why you'd want to keep that fact about yourself hidden. Last thing you needed was for your husband's colleagues or his voters to know about your dirt-poor roots. Of course, there was one man in your life who never cared about where you came from.

GRETCHEN. I'm sorry?

ARTHUR. The man who gave you the necklace. I believe you said his name was … Ted. Ted Randall.

GRETCHEN. Listen, I know I've been a bit distracted

lately, but I know well enough that I never mentioned Ted. Have you been going through my things while I've been asleep? *(No response.)* I think this conversation is over. *(She rises and heads for the hallway door. Arthur picks up the mirror, grabs his cane, and rises.)*

ARTHUR. Gretchen! You might want to take a look at this. *(She turns and stares into the mirror. Arthur hands it to her. She becomes transfixed by the sight.)*

GRETCHEN. *(Into mirror.)* Oh, look at me! This is the way I looked when I danced.

ARTHUR. You know, you could dance again. Right now, that is.

GRETCHEN. What? No, there's no way I could. Not like this.

ARTHUR. Sure, there is. Just stare into the mirror and imagine Ted Randall is watching. He had a pet-name for you, didn't he?

GRETCHEN. *(Lovingly.)* Butterfly Wings. He always said I came out fluttering like I had a pair of butterfly wings on my back.

ARTHUR. *(Into the mirror.)* So, dance, Butterfly Wings. The stage is yours. *(He turns on the radio. The same instrumental ballet music that played earlier begins to play. Gretchen does her best to recreate the dance she did as a ballerina. She watches herself in the mirror as she dances, growing more and more entranced by what she sees.)*

GRETCHEN. *(Into mirror.)* Look at my hair. Look at my body! *(Arthur turns up the volume as the music reaches its climax. As Gretchen finishes, she stares into the mirror with profound joy. Suddenly, the sound of thunderous applause is heard, prompting her to look around for the source. Arthur shuts off the radio and the applause fades.)* I think I … I need to sit down.

ARTHUR. *(Gestures to a seat.)* After a performance like that, it's understandable. *(Nods to mirror.)* Why, I got tired myself watching you. *(Arthur and Gretchen retake their seats.)*

GRETCHEN. That was the last song I ever danced to. I was set to have surgery on my ankles in the spring, so I knew when I danced that night, it would be my last time on stage.

ARTHUR. I bet you gave it your all. Especially since there was a special someone watching in the audience.

GRETCHEN. *(Twiddles her necklace.)* Ted had given me this a week prior. That night he was in his usual seat in the second to last row.

ARTHUR. *(Smiles.)* I was talking about Chuck. He was at that performance too. That's how the two of you met, wasn't it?

GRETCHEN. He had just announced his candidacy for mayor and was sitting in the front row. He came backstage and introduced himself after the performance.

ARTHUR. And a few weeks later, you called off the engagement to Ted and starting dating Chuck. *(Chuckles.)* I see how it is.

GRETCHEN. No, you don't! It was nothing like that. *(She looks down at the mirror only to become disappointed by what she sees. She shakes the handle and taps the frame.)*

ARTHUR. Is it being stubborn again? *(Gretchen nods and sets down the mirror in frustration.)*

GRETCHEN. I did not cheat on Ted with Chuck. Ted and I had been having problems for a while. He was always in-between jobs, and I was about to lose my career. I couldn't go back to the life I had had growing up. I couldn't go back to spending every day worrying about food and money.

ARTHUR. And then as if by magic, the answer to your prayers presented itself in the front row. This handsome, charismatic man with all the stability Ted lacked came out of nowhere and swept you off your feet.

GRETCHEN. After I met Chuck, I was going to galas and parties, and meeting the kinds of people I had always admired.

ARTHUR. A far cry from the farm girl who had to wear used overalls to school every day.

GRETCHEN. I did love, Chuck. When he asked me to marry him on election night, it was like a dream come true.

ARTHUR. Dreams are wonderful things, aren't they? Their only downside is sooner or later, you have to wake up. Tell me, when did you wake up, Gretchen?

GRETCHEN. Much sooner than I would have liked. Once he became mayor, I was required to live up to a certain level of standards. He dictated everything, but I kept telling myself, no matter how controlling he got, something greater was coming. I kept telling myself, no matter how bad things got, it would be worth it in the end.

ARTHUR. If I recall all the political pundits were predicting great things for Chuck. They were saying he could become a future governor, heck, maybe even a future President. *(Amused.)* Gretchen Hunter: First Lady of the United States. That's a dream no farm girl would ever want to wake up from. *(She takes it in for a moment.)* When was he officially diagnosed with Alzheimer's?

GRETCHEN. About six weeks after he announced he was running for governor. He fired all his assistants right after the diagnosis too. He wanted me, just me, to be his caregiver.

ARTHUR. All those years being told what to say, what to do, and in the end, your life was reduced to doing one thankless chore after another. Just like it was on that farm. And then one terrible morning you woke up and realized you had thrown away the one person who had truly loved you. *(Gestures to necklace.)* It explains why you started wearing Ted's necklace again. *(Pulls out pill bottle from garbage can.)* And why you took up some of your old habits.

GRETCHEN. I haven't taken up anything. Didn't you notice the bottle's in the trash? Didn't you notice it's empty?

ARTHUR. Seems pretty full to me. *(Rattles the bottle.)* Why if the whale who had swallowed Jonah had swallowed these instead, he would've been skinnier than a guppy fish! *(Gretchen snatches the bottle, opens it, and pours some diet pills into her palm.)*

GRETCHEN. No. I tossed these out into the snow. I threw them away.

ARTHUR. Certainly wouldn't be the first time you've imagined something. *(Mimics a voice that could resemble Gretchen's husband.)* "You keep popping those pills, Gretch, and you'll fry whatever's left of that tiny brain of yours! Why can't you lose weight like a normal person? Are you telling me you're too lazy to plop on the floor and do some pushups?"

GRETCHEN. STOP IT! *(She throws the pills onto the couch. Arthur rises with his cane. He clears his throat, and his voice returns to normal.)*

ARTHUR. Tell me, did Chuck really fall down the stairs? *(Smiles.)* You try to hide it, but it shows.

GRETCHEN. *(Stares into his eyes.)* You have his eyes. The same eyes that looked up at me that night … right before he … I did not murder my husband. Do you hear me? I did not murder him!

ARTHUR. I never said you did. Nah, I'm guessing what happened to Chuck was an accident. You probably came in late after a night of bar hopping, and there he was on the landing.

GRETCHEN. I was taken aback because he never stayed up that late. Not since he had been diagnosed. I ran up as fast as I could, but once I got up to the landing he started yelling.

ARTHUR. *(Sets down his cane.)* Yes, I reckon he must've said something that pushed you over the edge. He must've grabbed you too. *(Grabs her arms.)* And he must've gotten a good look at the necklace. *(Clears his throat.)* If I had to guess, I'd say he said something along the lines of … *(Mimics a voice that could resemble Gretchen's husband.)* "Where on earth you get this cheap thing, Gretch? Was it from that guy? You know, the one you were sleeping with before we met? That ugly, low-class, white trash bum who was just as poor and stupid as you were!?"

GRETCHEN. YOU SON OF A BITCH! *(She shoves him. Arthur falls to the ground laughing. He uses his cane to pick himself back up.)*

ARTHUR. I see we have our answer! *(He crosses to the armchair and sits. Gretchen collapses on the couch.)*

GRETCHEN. When I shoved him, I thought he'd fall backwards towards the bedroom. I never thought he'd fall the other way and … *(Struggles to compose herself.)* By the time I ran down it was already too late. As he lay there, he took my hand, and he tried to tell me something. But before he could finish it, he … he was gone.

ARTHUR. And did you tell the boys in blue any of this?

GRETCHEN. You know if I did, I wouldn't be sitting here right now.

ARTHUR. No, you'd be sitting in a big ole jail cell. Which leaves one lingering question. Given your history with Chuck, why would you want to go to his sister's for the holidays? Wait. Were you gonna tell her the truth and confess?

GRETCHEN. I couldn't take it. I couldn't take seeing him every time I went down the stairs. Besides, she has the right to know what happened. She has the right to know. *(Picks up a diet pill and stares at it.)* "It's never too late to do the right thing." Ted used to tell me that. *(She picks up the mirror and stares at her reflection. Disappointed.)* It's still not working.

ARTHUR. While we wait for it to work again, how's about we play a little game? It'll work like this. I'll try to guess what Chuck was trying to tell you in his final moments, and you say whether you think I'm right or not.

GRETCHEN. You want to try and guess what my husband was trying to tell me right before he died? Do you have any idea how sick that sounds?

ARTHUR. *(Gestures to mirror.)* No sicker than the game you're trying to play with that thing.

GRETCHEN. *(Sets down mirror.)* All right. Go ahead.

ARTHUR. I'm willing to bet Chuck was trying to say he never loved you. He was trying to say he needed a wife to advance his political career, and that every minute of your marriage was based off that need.

GRETCHEN. How dare you say that to me? HOW DARE YOU!

ARTHUR. You mean to tell me, in all those unhappy years, you never once questioned why he came to your performance with his campaign manager.

GRETCHEN. How do you know that? How did you know he came to the ballet with Rick?

ARTHUR. *(Smiles.)* Like I told you before, a magician never reveals his secrets.

GRETCHEN. *(looks him over)* Magician? I don't think so. I think you probably read about it in one of the papers. Yes, all the local ones ran stories on how we first met. One of them probably reported that he brought Rick along.

ARTHUR. And did any of the papers report what he was whispering to Rick while he watched you dance? You've always wondered that, haven't you? You've always wondered what he was saying to him as he watched you from seat A6.

GRETCHEN. Tell me. Tell me what he said. TELL ME NOW!

ARTHUR. *(Mimics a voice that could resemble Gretchen's husband.)* "The one twirling in the middle looks like a good bet. I can see all the papers now: "Mayoral candidate courts girl-next-door ballerina." The media will eat it up." *(Switches to voice that could resemble Rick.)* "You can't be serious, Chuck. We did our research. She came from a farm. Girl's a step above trailer-trash." *(Mimics a voice that could resemble Gretchen's husband.)* "All the better. Voters will love nothing more than a rags to riches story especially when the girl stands a chance at becoming the city's next first lady. Heck, if it works out, she could be on magazine covers someday. Well, as long as she keeps that gut under control." *(A long pause as his voice returns to normal.)* You know what happened next. After the show, Chuck came backstage and gave you his number. It was the same phone number you hid from Ted when he took you out for a celebratory dinner. It was at that dinner when he told you he had lost another job. But what you don't know is that while you and Teddy were sharing a cheap bottle of wine, Chuck and Rick were sharing a fine bottle of champagne and having a conversation of their own. *(Mimics a voice that could resemble Gretchen's husband.)* "You see how her eyes lit up when I gave her my number? Girl's begging for it. By the time we make our first campaign stop, she'll be all dolled up and ready to go." *(Switches to a voice that could resemble Rick.)* "I don't know about that. Didn't you see there was a guy waiting for her in the parking lot? I saw the way he kissed her. It looked pretty serious." *(Mimics a voice that could resemble Gretchen's husband.)* "This was the last performance of her career. She'll be looking for new ways to get attention. What better way than to date a future mayor. At the very least I'll get to have some fun in the sack. Did you see her body? You see how it moved? It's like she had a pair of butterfly wings attached to it or something." *(Gretchen rises from the couch and grabs a hold of him.)*

GRETCHEN. YOU BASTARD! I'm not sorry for what I did to you that night. You hear me? I'm glad you fell down the stairs. I'm glad you cracked your head open. I'M GLAD YOU'RE DEAD! *(A struggle ensues between the two. Gretchen falls to the floor. With a twitching hand, she reaches up and takes some diet pills off the cushions. She pops pill after pill into her mouth and takes a greedy gulp of brandy. She then picks up the mirror and becomes transfixed by what she sees.)* Oh…look at me. Look at Teddy! He's there too. I see him! *(The Upstage Left elevator doors open. After a few seconds, Gretchen becomes disappointed by what she sees in the mirror.)* Wait. I don't see anything now. There's not even a reflection of me anymore.

ARTHUR. There are plenty more mirrors downstairs. Why don't you head on down and grab one? *(He gestures to the elevator. Gretchen prepares to set down the mirror.)* No, take it with you. It usually grants guests one final surprise on their way down. *(She crosses to the elevator with the mirror in hand. She steps through the doors.)*

GRETCHEN. *(Searches the walls.)* Is there a button or do theses doors close automatically? *(Looks at mirror.)* Hey, it's working again. I'm starting to see a reflection! *(Examines the reflection.)* Wait. I'm old. Older than I am now. My hair, my face, my … body … they're burning. THEY'RE COVERED IN FIRE! *(She attempts to exit the elevator only to crumble to the floor. She clutches her stomach and screams.)* Help me! I can't breathe. I can't breathe. GOD, HELP ME! *(Arthur raises the shot glass of bourbon as if to propose a toast.)*

ARTHUR. He can't help you now, sweetheart. No one can. *(The lights flash red and flicker as the elevator doors begin to close. By the time the doors fully close and stifle the last of Gretchen's screams, Arthur downs his shot of bourbon. The lights continue to flicker until they BLACKOUT. After a few moments, the lights go back up to reveal Arthur standing with his cane in hand. He sets down the empty shot glass and crosses to the elevator doors. He presses the button causing the Upstage Left doors to open. Gretchen is nowhere to be found and her clothes lie in a heap on the floor. Arthur picks up her clothes, crosses to the coffee table, and drops them on its surface. He rummages through them while the Upstage Right elevator doors open. The Stranger enters. She has become visibly older and walks with the assistance of a cane. She staggers to the couch. The elevator doors close behind her.)* Ah. I was wondering when you'd show up. *(The Stranger collapses onto the couch, gasping for breath. She flips over her arms. Her skin is covered in green scales.)*

THE STRANGER. *(Staggers for breath.)* What … what is happening? What did you do to me?

ARTHUR. I didn't do anything to you. You did this to yourself when you agreed to our deal. *(He withdraws the document from his pocket and places it before her.)* Remember how you noticed a smudge next to one of the conditions? I'm afraid it wasn't a smudge. It was an asterisk. Flip it over and read. *(The Stranger turns over the document.)*

THE STRANGER. *(Reads out loud.)* "In the event Mr. Arthur Nelligan claims all the participants, the signer of this document will ..."

ARTHUR. Finish it.

THE STRANGER. "Be claimed by Mr. Arthur Nelligan as well."

ARTHUR. A fine example of why you should never sign a document until you've read the entire thing. Front and back.

THE STRANGER. *(Sets down the document.)* This isn't over yet. Do you hear me?

ARTHUR. Oh, I hear ya, sweetheart, loud and clear. It's just a shame you haven't heard the latest news. *(He reaches under the coffee table and pulls out the newspaper.)* From yesterday's paper. I think you'll find the obituary section particularly interesting. *(The Stranger snatches the paper, turns to the appropriate section, and silently reads.)*

THE STRANGER. *(Defeated.)* No. No ... *(Arthur crosses to the coat rack.)*

ARTHUR. I was surprised he didn't bother to tell you. Especially since this changes everything. *(The Stranger sets down the paper and rises with her cane. She crosses to Arthur who gestures to the red suite with the black tie.)* What do ya think? I know it's not exactly a coat of many colors, but I think it'll do just fine and dandy when I walk out that door. *(No response.)* I must say, you're taking this rather well. I expected more of a reaction from you. I expected fear, sorrow ... rage.

THE STRANGER. "Fools give full vent to their rage, but the wise bring calm in the end."

ARTHUR. Perhaps, I should give you a little preview of what's to come by this time tomorrow night. *(Sets down cane.)* It'll begin with a fall into a deep abyss. *(Without warning, he kicks her cane away, causing her to fall to the floor. He then climbs atop of her, grabs her arms, and pins them above her head.)* An abyss so cold you will lose all perception of time. From there, you will land in a barren wasteland where the darkness is so consuming, you'll forget everything about yourself. You will lose your senses, and you will crawl. You will crawl in every direction imaginable, because in the end, you'll believe if you just keep crawling, you'll reach some sort of end. But just when you think you've reached it, that is when you will slither into fire. *(Leans in and whispers.)* And as you plead for mercy, as you beg for relief, I will emerge from the flames, and I will smile upon you. For you will have finally rendered yourself onto me. Our relationship will end the way it was supposed to begin. With you by side before you betrayed me for him. Tell me, where is he in your hour of need? Where is he with all his power? *(He licks the side of her face causing her to scream in protest. When he is satisfied, he rises. The Stranger crawls upon the floor only for her strength to fail her. BLACKOUT. After a few seconds, the lights come back up again. The Stranger has vanished. Arthur hobbles over to Gretchen's clothes without the assistance of the cane. He picks up a pair of underwear.)* You know, Gretch, from the moment you walked through my door, I had a feeling I'd be getting into your panties. *(He discards the underwear and pulls out a snake.)* My, my, my! Aint you a beauty. *(He crosses to the snake cage. His hobble improves with each step. Upon reaching the cage, he tosses the snake inside. He then withdraws his pocket watch and examines the time.)* Six minutes past midnight. December 24th. All that's left is the prodigal. *(The snakes within the cage hiss.)* "I am the Alpha and the Omega. Who is, and who was, and who is to come, the Almighty." *(He smiles in delight. The lights go down.)*

End of scene.

ACT TWO
Scene 3

The lounge of the Nelligan Motel.

The next morning. December 24th.

Marilyn paces back and forth with her cell phone. She searches for a signal. A discarded breakfast tray rests on the coffee table beside her purse, satchel, and suitcase. The radio plays.

VOICE ON THE RADIO (V.O). All major roads have been cleared, providing some much needed relief for travelers on this Christmas Eve. And now back to another segment of commercial-free music. *(Marilyn shuts off the radio and goes to put the phone inside her purse when she notices something. She reaches inside and pulls out the tourniquet. She crosses to the garbage can. Unbeknownst to her, Arthur enters from the hallway door. He looks even younger and walks without a hobble. He carries a newspaper. After a moment of contemplation, Marilyn tosses the tourniquet into the garbage can. She then notices Arthur.)*

MARILYN. Oh, good morning, Arthur! *(Observes him.)* I see you're walking without your cane now. Makes you look even younger than yesterday!

ARTHUR. You're too kind. I'm gonna miss ya when you leave.

MARILYN. I'm not sure I will be leaving. Landline in my room is still dead.

ARTHUR. *(Gestures to newspaper.)* Morning paper said a lot of the phone lines are still down. I'd try your cell again. Gretchen was able to get a signal earlier.

MARILYN. Are you saying she's gone now too?

ARTHUR. *(Gestures to notebook.)* Checked out around six.

MARILYN. That's too bad. She gave me some money yesterday. I would've liked to have thanked her again.

ARTHUR. I wouldn't worry about it. I have a feeling you'll be seeing her again soon. *(Gestures to phone.)* Want me to try and get you a signal?

MARILYN. Knock yourself out. *(Arthur sets down the newspaper on the counter and takes her phone. He crosses behind the counter.)*

ARTHUR. Now Gretchen was able to get service right around here … *(Holds the phone up and stops in a specific spot.)* Well, I'll be. I think I got something. *(Shows her the screen.)* I'll call you a taxi. *(Arthur dials a number. Marilyn pages through the newspaper.)* Hi, this is Arthur Nelligan at the Nelligan Motel. I need another taxi sent out here. Thank you. *(Marilyn stops at the obituary section as Arthur hands her back the phone.)* Should be here within the hour. The Nelligan Motel will be covering the fee of course.

MARILYN. Wow. Talk about an early gift! Thank you so much.

ARTHUR. It's not a gift. It's common courtesy. Something most people don't seem to have anymore. Now this is a gift. *(He reaches below and places a gift bag on the countertop.)* Go on. *(She reaches inside and pulls out a neatly bound, typed manuscript.)*

MARILYN. A book! Thank you. I've been meaning to catch up on some reading. I can start on the ride into the city … wait … *(Reads the cover.)* "The Adventures of Ariadne Longtail…by Marilyn Morris."

ARTHUR. It wasn't easy getting all that typed up. Especially the bits written on napkins. But I managed.

MARILYN. You typed up my book?

ARTHUR. I figured it'd be easier for your mother to read it this way. I left a page blank at the beginning.

MARILYN. *(Turns to the page.)* I see. What for?

ARTHUR. Isn't that where authors usually write out a dedication to someone?

MARILYN. You really thought of everything, didn't you? *(Examines book once more.)* Thank you. Thank you so much. *(Arthur picks up the pen beside the notebook and hands it to her. Marilyn takes the pen and begins to write out a dedication. Arthur crosses to the coffee table. He begins to tidy up the items left on the discarded breakfast tray.)*

ARTHUR. Is there anything else I can get you? *(She finishes writing and crosses to the coffee table with the book and pen. She sets down the book.)*

MARILYN. Between this and how you helped me when I wasn't … feeling myself, you've shown me more kindness these past few days than most people have shown me in years.

ARTHUR. Just don't go forgetting about me when you get that publishing deal.

MARILYN. I won't. I promise.

ARTHUR. Good. Now, I better get this place straightened up. *(He picks up the breakfast tray. Marilyn notices she still has the pen. She crosses to the counter. Upon setting down the pen, she notices the obituary page of the newspaper. She becomes alarmed.)*

MARILYN. What? *(Reads the page to herself.)* No … NO!

ARTHUR. Marilyn? Is something wrong? *(Marilyn struggles to compose herself. Arthur scoops up the paper.)*

ARTHUR. *(Reads.)* "Ruth Morris, age 66, passed away late Wednesday evening following a stroke. She is the widowed wife of Pittsburgh minister, Abraham Morris. An affluent member of the community, she was involved with many charity groups …" Oh, my. This wasn't your mother, was it?

MARILYN. *(Nods.)* We hadn't spoken in years, and now we'll never get another chance.

ARTHUR. My, my, my. I am so sorry. Is there anyone you'd like me to call for you? Siblings? Relatives?

MARILYN. I was her only child. I … I don't have any other family. I … I don't know where I'm supposed to go now.

ARTHUR. You listen to me. You are welcome to stay here as long as you need and at no charge.

MARILYN. *(Nods.)* I just need some time to myself right now.

ARTHUR. Of course. I'll leave you be. *(Marilyn crosses to the couch and sits. Arthur exits out the hallway door with the tray. Marilyn picks up the book, turns to the dedication page, and silently reads what she wrote moments prior. She loses all composure. Unbeknownst to her, the Upstage Right elevator doors open. The Stranger enters. She has aged even further and now walks with a walker. Her neck, cheeks, and arms are covered in sickly scales. The elevator doors close behind her and the lights flicker. Marilyn becomes alerted to her presence. She rises.)*

THE STRANGER. Don't be afraid, Marilyn. I'm here about your mother, Ruth.

MARILYN. Ruth Morris? You knew my mother?

THE STRANGER. I know your mother. She always supported you. Despite everything you did to her, including that night at the Granger Motel.

MARILYN. Who are you? How do you know about that

night?

THE STRANGER. If I explain, you'll never be able to save yourself.

MARILYN. Save myself from what?

THE STRANGER. From losing the only thing you have left. *(The lights flicker until they BLACKOUT. After a few seconds, the lights come up again. The Stranger has disappeared, and Marilyn now stands by herself. Confused, she frantically searches the room. Arthur reenters from the hallway door.)*

ARTHUR. Landline is working again. I called the taxi service and told them they're no longer needed.

MARILYN. Arthur, are you sure there's no one else here? Like an older woman with a walker?

ARTHUR. An older woman with a walker? Are you feeling well this morning, Marilyn? Minus the news about your mother of course. *(Touches her forehead.)* Oh my. You're burning up. Perhaps you should lie down. *(He removes his hand. Marilyn begins to tremble.)*

MARILYN. *(Nods.)* I'll get my room key.

ARTHUR. I'm afraid I haven't cleaned the rooms yet. *(Gestures to couch.)* Why don't you rest out here for the time being? *(She nods again and curls up on the couch. Arthur crosses to the coatrack and removes his red suit and black tie. He crosses to the hallway door and watches Marilyn close her eyes. With a smile.)* I'll see you later … *(He turns off the light switch on the wall and exits.)*

 End of scene.

ACT TWO
Scene 4

The lounge of the Nelligan Motel.

Later that evening.

Marilyn has fallen asleep and is curled up on the couch. As she sleeps, the radio spring to life by itself.

VOICE ON THE RADIO (V.O). … with power fully restored across the area, thousands of families are now free to enjoy each other's company on this wintery Christmas Eve.

MARILYN. *(Talking in her sleep.)* Mom! *(A Christmas song plays. Marilyn jolts awake and examines her surroundings. She touches her forehead and notices her hands shake. She rises and rushes over to the bar cart. She grabs hold of the thermos and goes to drink from it, only to discover it is empty. She grows physically ill.)* Not again. *(She struggles to catch her breath. Arthur calmly enters from the hallway wearing the red suit and black tie. He crosses to the radio and turns it off.)*

ARTHUR. Hello, Sleepy-Head. 'Bout time you opened your eyes.

MARILYN. What time is it?

ARTHUR. *(Reveals a pocket watch.)* Quarter to midnight. That was quite the nap.

MARILYN. Arthur, I really need some more of that apple juice.

ARTHUR. I'm afraid I'm all out. I didn't bother to make any more because you seemed to be doing so much … better.

MARILYN. Please. I'm sick and I need some. *(He crosses to the bar cart and withdraws the bottle of bourbon and a shot glass. He brings them over to the armchair and sets them down on the stand.)*

ARTHUR. Maybe you don't. Maybe it's all in your head like one of those bad dreams you were having. I heard you screaming over one earlier. I was tempted to wake you, but you finally snapped out of it. I could be wrong, but it sounded like you were mumbling something about a Granger Motel. Is that out in Los Angeles?

MARILYN. *(Covers her mouth.)* I'm gonna puke. *(She rushes to the garbage can and falls to her knees.)*

ARTHUR. Goodness gracious. Cut that out. Here, let me help you. *(He helps her to her feet and caresses her stomach and arms. As if by magic, she stops trembling.)* See? All you have to do is trust me. *(He kisses her forehead and takes a seat in the armchair. Marilyn sits on the couch. She touches her forehead and notices the sweat is gone. After a moment, she speaks.)*

MARILYN. The Granger Motel isn't in Los Angeles. It's from around here. It's about a half hour from where I grew up.

ARTHUR. I see. Well, given the way you were carrying on about it, I'll be sure to avoid it at all costs.

MARILYN. *(A moment.)* A guy beat me up there once.

ARTHUR. I beg your pardon.

MARILYN. It was right after I was told I wouldn't be graduating high school. I got into this huge fight with my mother. She was furious and I said some really horrible things to her. I then drove off with this guy I knew. He didn't have a home to go to, so he drove us to the Granger Motel where we could be alone and talk. I told him everything that had happened, and within minutes he had pulled out every drug imaginable for us to try. After that, he told me how he really felt about me. He made a move, but I told him I wasn't interested. Next thing I knew, I was on the floor with a mouth full of blood. He punched, he kicked, but before he could go any further, an employee banged on the door. I was too drugged out of my mind to form a sentence, so while he was busy at the door, I slid out a back window and took off. I ran and I ran, until a police car pulled up beside me.

ARTHUR. Police must've had a field day when they arrested him. *(Silence.)* They did arrest him, didn't they?

MARILYN. After I was taken to the hospital, they asked me who had beaten me up. I was about to tell them the truth, when I thought about the fight I had had with my mom. I felt so ashamed, so disgusted that all the things she had predicted about my life were slowly coming true. I wanted to hurt her, the way I had been hurting ever since my dad died.

ARTHUR. You told them it was you mother. You told them your mother had beaten you up, didn't you? *(Marilyn breaks down and nods.)* My, my, my …

MARILYN. I dropped the charges, but that was the last we ever spoke. After that, I lived with a friend who introduced me to that theatre director. After the play failed, the director and I moved to L.A. for a fresh start. But once we got there and the rejections came, we found ourselves turning to something I had experience with.

ARTHUR. I take it this something was administered via needle. I can only imagine what a young vulnerable woman like you had to do to make ends meet. But what about Mr. Theatre Director? What did he have to do?

MARILYN. He went through whatever money we had, including some money I had inherited from my father. *(Composes herself.)* In the end he left me, got the help he needed, and actually made something of himself. I know because I slept under a marquee with his name on it one night.

ARTHUR. Tell me, Marilyn, how does one go from sleeping under marquees and living by the needle, to becoming an aspiring novelist on her way home for the holidays?

MARILYN. One night, a man pulled up and offered me double my usual rate. I accepted and he drove us to some apartment on the other side of the city. When we got there, he told me he had killed a man in prison, and that he had just been paid forty grand to murder some guy's wife. I got scared, but before I could leave, he pulled out a knife, held it to my throat, and forced himself on me. Through it all, he pinched the marks on my arms and made me repeat the things the woman had said to him as he had stabbed her to death. When he was done, he looked out the window and saw his parole officer pulling up for an unannounced visit. I begged him to pay me something, anything, even if it was just five bucks, but he said he would slit my throat if I didn't get out. It was raining hard that night and my cell was dead, so I began to run. I ran until I twisted my ankle and fell into a puddle of filth. I lay there, trembling and sobbing, until someone finally came over and helped me. When I got back on my feet, I looked into the puddle and saw a woman who looked more like an animal than a human being. I was repulsed by the woman's appearance, disgusted that someone could look like that, until I realized the woman was me. By the time I got to the police, I couldn't remember where the man's apartment had been. All I knew was I had to go home to the one person who knew me, the real me, and not the person who didn't even recognize her own reflection. I saved whatever I could, even if it was pennies in the gutter, and when I finally had enough, I stuffed what I had into a suitcase and took the first bus out of the city. Through it all, no matter how sick I got, no matter how much I needed a fix, I focused on writing the book I had always wanted to write. And while I wrote it for my father, I wrote it for my mother too. I wrote it for her, so that when she saw me again, she would see it was possible for me to do something good. She would see it was possible for me to become the woman she had tried to raise. *(Arthur pulls out the book from her satchel. He reads the dedication page.)*

ARTHUR. "To my mother, Ruth. Thank you for being the person I still aspire to be. Love, Marilyn." *(Sets down the book.)* I wish she could've seen this, especially since you prayed for it on your way out here.

MARILYN. How did you know that? How did you know I started praying again?

ARTHUR. Because I heard your prayers, Marilyn. I heard the ones you said from the park benches, and I heard the ones you said from the homeless shelters. I heard them all, just like I heard the ones you said when you were begging your God to save your father. *(Puts his hands together and mimics a little girl's voice.)* "Please God. Don't let my daddy die. I promise, I'll be good for Mommy. I won't be bad for her ever again. Please just save my Daddy. I need him."

MARILYN. Arthur, I don't know what's going on here, but it's really starting to scare me.

ARTHUR. *(Voice returns to normal.)* Then perhaps it's time you learned the truth.

MARILYN. What're you talking about? What truth?

ARTHUR. The same truth I hid from Tom and Gretchen. You yourself weren't ready to hear it earlier, but I'm confident you're ready to hear it now. *(He crosses to the radio and plays with the dials.)* This aired the day after you arrived. It should explain everything. *(The Voice on the Radio speaks.)*

VOICE ON THE RADIO (V.O). ...passengers included Tom Gavin, a serial thief wanted across multiple states, Gretchen Hunter, former First Lady of Pittsburgh, and Marilyn Morris, a known Los Angeles prostitute. All three were killed in yesterday's horrific bus crash. The bus driver remains in critical condition. We repeat, Tom Gavin, Gretchen Hunter, and Marilyn Morris have been confirmed dead. Stay tuned for further updates. *(Arthur turns off the radio. He crosses to the armchair, reaches under it, and pulls out the front page to a newspaper.)*

MARILYN. No, that's ... that's not possible. The bus only skidded off the road. We were fine. I was fine.

ARTHUR. *(Hands her newspaper page.)* If it's any consolation, none of you suffered.

MARILYN. *(Reads page to herself.)* No. NO! I am not dead. Do you hear me? I AM NOT DEAD! *(She throws down the page and races to the front door. She flings it open and exits. Arthur pours himself a shot of bourbon)*

ARTHUR. In three ... two ... one ... *(The door bursts open and Marilyn collapses onto the floor. She gasps for air. Arthur crosses to the front door and closes it.)* You can run out there as many times as you'd like. In the end, the world of the living will always reject you.

MARILYN. Where am I? What is this place?

ARTHUR. It's a place for those just like you. A place for those in search of what comes next. You see Marilyn, just like Tom, Gretchen, and countless others, you now have a choice as to what happens next. Keep in mind, I can guide you as best I can, but in the end, you're the one who ultimately decides your fate.

MARILYN. What exactly are you, Arthur? Are you some kind of … of …?

ARTHUR. Some kind of what?

MARILYN. Angel?

ARTHUR. *(Smiles.)* I was…once. Over the years, I've gone by many names for I was present when the earth began. I've soared above your skies as an angel, and I've walked among your people as a charming stranger. Through it all, mankind has looked to me for guidance, and has often turned to me as a last resort. As of now, I am whatever you need me to be, Marilyn Morris, for I alone can assist you in your hour of need. *(Marilyn looks into his eyes and takes a step back.)* You can see it in my eyes now, can't you? You can see I'm telling you the truth. There's no reason to fear me. All I've ever wanted was to give a second chance to those who've deserved it.

MARILYN. A second chance at what?

ARTHUR. In your case, a second chance at life. Rest assured; it would be good one. A happy one. The kind your parents always wanted for you. If you'd like a preview as to what it includes, all you need to do is look in your satchel. *(Marilyn reaches into her satchel and pulls out a professionally produced hard cover novel.)*

MARILYN. This is my book. *(Reads the cover.)* It's published and it's…an international bestseller. *(Arthur takes the book.)*

ARTHUR. If you pledge yourself to me, not only will this object become a reality, but so will your second chance. All the pain, sorrow, and unhappiness you felt in your old life will cease to exist. In this new life, no needle will ever pierce your veins, and the only men who will touch you, will do so out of love and respect. I can perform miracles too, and unlike the God your parents worshipped, I honor those who are loyal to me. Those that pledge themselves to me will never be abandoned. Not even to death. Let me save you, Marilyn. Let me save you the way I could've saved your mother and your father.

MARILYN. You could've saved them?

ARTHUR. Especially your father. Do you know how painful it was for me to hear his prayers and to know there was nothing I could do to help him? All he ever wanted was to be there for you while you were growing up. When you look at that and compare it to all the other things people ask for, it wasn't that much of a request. *(Nods to the front door.)* Do you know how many murderers are out there right now? How many rapists? How many child molesters? Because I can tell you the exact number. I can also tell you how many of them will go unpunished and live happy lives. The same can't be said for good, decent people like your parents.

MARILYN. You said someone like me had a choice. You said what will happen if I pledge myself to you. What will happen if I don't?

ARTHUR. I'm afraid, you'll simply fade away into nothing.

MARILYN. No … NO!

ARTHUR. Given the life you lived and all the terrible things you did to yourself and to those who loved you, did you really expect anything different? I can answer your prayers, Marilyn, but first you need to trust me. The question now is, will you? *(He offers her the published book. Marilyn stares at it. After much deliberation, she takes it. The Upstage Left elevator doors open.)*

MARILYN. *(Gestures to front door.)* Will we be heading out there together?

ARTHUR. Of course. But before we do, there are a few more copies of your book down in the basement. Why don't you head on down and get them? I'll wait for you. *(Marilyn nods and crosses to the open elevator. Arthur basks in triumph and downs the shot of bourbon. He then crosses to the front door and opens it. He pulls out the pocket watch.)* Not even midnight yet! I tell ya, we're making excellent time. *(He eagerly waits to cross the threshold. Marilyn approaches the elevator.)* Mark my words, that book is just the beginning. I'll make sure that play of yours gets recognition too. Heck, I already see it getting standing ovations on Broadway! *(Marilyn stops just as she is about to enter the elevator. A moment passes.)* Is something wrong?

MARILYN. It was my mother.

ARTHUR. Excuse me.

MARILYN. *(Turns back to Arthur.)* My mother came to my play that night. She was the one who stood in the back of the theatre and clapped. Despite everything I did to her, she still came out to support me. If I had known that, if I had known she still loved me, I never would've left. I would've gone home to her instead. She would've been there for me. She would've helped me.

ARTHUR. That's all very sweet, but it doesn't matter what could've been. All that matters is what can happen now. And right now, I am offering you this second chance. Trust me, it's what your mother and father would have wanted.

MARILYN. Would they? Like this, I mean … *(She contemplates as she turns to the book. She opens it and pages through it.)* This isn't even my book. It's just pages of scribbles. *(Arthur slams the front door shut in disgust. He throws the pocket watch on the couch and crosses to the garbage can.)*

ARTHUR. You want to know how your mother died? She died twitching on the floor with a rosary in her hand. That's what your God thought of her. She suffered a cruel and sadistic end, just like your father did, and just like you will now if you turn away from me. The only difference is you'll suffer with an old friend. *(He reaches into the garbage can and pulls out a heroin needle. Marilyn recoils.)*

MARILYN. *(Mumbles.)* "Yea, though I walk through the valley of the shadow of death, I will fear no evil…"

ARTHUR. *(Smiles.)* Prayers aren't gonna help you now, sweetheart. They didn't help your father either. *(Mimics a voice that could resemble Marilyn's father.)* "Lord, in my entire life, I've never asked you for much, but I'm begging you for something now. Please, let me live. Let me live for my Marilyn."

MARILYN. No. No, I can't.

ARTHUR. *(Mimics a voice that could resemble Marilyn's father.)* "She needs her daddy. Without me, she'll fall apart."

MARILYN. Stop it.

ARTHUR. *(Mimics a voice that could resemble Marilyn's father.)* "I promise, I will continue to spread your sacred word. (Starts to gasp for breath.) Let me live for Marilyn. Please … please …"

MARILYN. STOP IT! *(She collapses in a heap before the snake cage and sobs. Arthur pulls her up and presses her into the cage. His voice returns to normal.)*

ARTHUR. Is this what you want, Marilyn? *(Grinds against her.)* To spend your final moments of existence as a drug-addicted harlot? *(He takes her hand and places the heroin needle in it. As if under a spell, Marilyn instinctively brings the needle towards her arm. She struggles against it.)* To fade without meaning? To die without purpose just like your father did. *(The room fills with the hiss of snakes. Marilyn continues to struggle against the needle. After a long moment, she forces herself to look him in the eyes.)*

MARILYN. There was a purpose.

ARTHUR. What?

MARILYN. My father died saving me, so that one day, I would be strong enough to save myself. If I fade into nothing, then so be it. But before I do, I want to say how sorry I am for all the horrible things I've done. And I want to reject you and everything you stand for. *(She wins the battle against the needle.)*

ARTHUR. No. NO! You will not cheat me. YOU WILL NOT CHEAT ME! *(He goes to grab her by the throat. Before he gets the chance, Marilyn thrusts the needle into his stomach. Arthur staggers backward as a series of white lights flash across the room. He then falls to the floor and begins to convulse. The Upstage Right elevator doors open to reveal The Stranger. Her snake scales are gone, and she looks as youthful as she did at the beginning of the play. She scoops up the pocket watch from the couch and approaches Marilyn.)*

MARILYN. *(To The Stranger.)* It's you.

THE STRANGER. Yes. I am as I should be. As are you. *(She turns Marilyn's arms over to reveal the needle marks are gone. She then examines the pocket watch.)* Midnight on the dot.

MARILYN. December 25th. *(Beams in triumph.)* Merry Christmas.

THE STRANGER. *(Smiles.)* Merry Christmas, Marilyn. Your mother and father are waiting for you. Would you like to see them? *(Marilyn eagerly nods and follows her across the room. Arthur rips the needle out from his stomach. He attempts to rise, but his legs no longer have the strength.)*

ARTHUR. Marilyn, you need me. YOU NEED ME! *(He falls to his knees before the garbage can. The Stranger points to the radio. Religious Christmas music begins to play. Arthur grabs hold of the garbage can and vomits. Marilyn and The Stranger enter the elevator hand in hand.)* YOU. NEED. ME! *(The music grows louder and louder. As the elevator doors close on Marilyn and The Stranger, Arthur releases an agonizing scream in defeat.)*

End of scene.

ACT TWO
Scene 5

The lounge of the motel.

New Year's Eve.

The snake cage has been removed. A bottle of white wine, a wine glass, a bottle of bourbon, and a shot glass have been placed on the coffee table. Garland has been strung across the counter. A Christmas tree has been set up near the front door. The radio plays the song, Auld Lang Sang. The Stranger enters through the hallway door. She carries a nativity set over to the table. She sets it up. The Upstage Left elevator doors open to reveal Arthur. He walks with his walker and appears as he did at the beginning of the play. The elevator doors close behind him as he crosses to the coffee table. He struggles to get himself situated in one of the chairs.

THE STRANGER. Ah. I was wondering when you'd show up. *(Observes Arthur struggling.)* Need any assistance?

ARTHUR. Right now, I just need the drink. *(He finally sits. The Stranger crosses to the coffee table and sits in the chair opposite him. They both pour themselves drinks. Arthur sips from his shot glass.)*

THE STRANGER. How is it?

ARTHUR. Like I remember. Wish I could say the same for

the rest of this place. *(He pulls out the deck of cards from his pocket. He shuffles the deck and divides it in two. He keeps one half for himself, and hands the other half to her. Looks around the room at the décor.)* Isn't it a little late for decorations?

THE STRANGER. There are twelve days of Christmas, and New Year's Eve is one of them. It's still the season to be jolly. *(They begin to play a round of war with the cards.)*

ARTHUR. Yes, I imagine you and everyone else up there have been extra jolly lately.

THE STRANGER. You were able to claim two new souls and yet you're still miserable. Why is that? *(Takes a moment to think and then smiles.)* Because you can't stop thinking about her. You can't stop thinking about the one who slipped through your fingers, can you? *(Collects some cards.)* She's doing great by the way. So are her parents.

ARTHUR. Same can't be said for Tom, Gretchen, and all the others.

THE STRANGER. Spin the situation however you want. You failed. You didn't get what you wanted.

ARTHUR. For now. *(Collects some cards.)* I reckon you finally settled on an alias.

THE STRANGER. Hope. It's what I renamed the place as well. From now on, lost souls will be staying at the Hope Motel. *(The Stranger will now be referred to as HOPE. Arthur downs the rest of his shot glass.)*

ARTHUR. *(Examines empty shot glass.)* You know, if this wasn't the good stuff, I'd puke it up right now.

HOPE. Give yourself time. After all, you've got plenty of it.

ARTHUR. Yes. Your precious God made sure to remind me. *(He raises a leg of his pants. A new ankle bracelet rests above the old one.)* But like us, he knows this is all far from over. Tell me, what does a lifetime for me in here, translate to out there? *(Gestures to front door.)* Seconds? Minutes? An hour at most? You can't keep me locked up in here forever. Sooner or later, I will be able to walk the world of the living as I please. And if you can't claim all the lost souls within this purgatory, what chance do you stand of claiming them all out there?

HOPE. *(Smiles.)* I could ask you the same question. *(She notices they each have the same number of cards.)* We're going to be at this for a long time, aren't we?

ARTHUR. Longer than either of us care to admit. *(Hope reaches into her pocket and pulls out the pocket watch.)*

HOPE. Less than a minute to midnight now. *(She pours herself another glass of wine. Arthur pours himself another shot of bourbon.)* Heaven knows I've made plenty of resolutions for the new year.

ARTHUR. As have I. And I'm gonna have a hell of a time fulfilling each and every one of them. *(Raises his shot glass.)* Shall we make a toast? *(Hope raises her wine glass.)*

HOPE. To the New Year. *(A series of knocks comes from the front door. Hope and Arthur look to the door and then to each other.)*

ARTHUR. And to second chances. *(He clangs the shot glass against her wine glass and downs its contents with a sinister grin.)*

END OF PLAY

NOTES
(Use this space to make notes for your production)

NOTES
(Use this space to make notes for your production)

84

BOBBY IS DEAD

by Marty Matfess

2M, 3W, DARK COMEDY

Chris has been madly in love with his best friend Annie for years, but she's only been interested in dating everyone else but him. After Annie's recent break up with her boyfriend Bobby, Chris feels this may finally be what he needs to find his way into her heart, but just like that ... she's already moved on to another guy she met at a coffee shop. Being the good friend that he is, Chris has agreed to hang out with the new guy's visiting sister while they go out on a date. Oh, and let's not forget about Bobby. Turns out he's not taking the break up too well and Chris is now in the midst of an aggressive ex-boyfriend while having to keep new guy's sister company. A play about love, lust, and getting shot in the head.

IN THE SLUSH

by Daniel Prillaman

2M, 2W, HORROR

2023 FINALIST FOR NEW DRAMATISTS' PRINCESS GRACE AWARD

Newlywed Laura Beth Gardner has it all. A loving husband, a baby on the way, and a usually delightful job. But this weekend, tasked with reading through her publishing house's slush pile, she encounters a mysterious manuscript that claims she isn't human. That her husband isn't who he says he is. And that she's a vessel for her unborn child, who is actually the Second Coming of an ancient darkness that will devour the world. It has to be some sort of joke. …But what if it's not?

A cosmic horror about identity, creation, and the things we'll do to realize our dreams.

KINGDUMB

by Jonathan Cook

10M, 6W, COMEDY

There's a new King in the land that has initiated a mysterious new tax on the citizens. Outraged, the region's finest Clock fixer, aka "Time Repair Specialist", recruits some of the most unlikely rebels to help him develop a plan to overthrow the King. Their plotting takes them on a comedic journey through perilous mountain tops all the way to the palace itself where they confront this vile King face to face. Kingdumb is a medieval fantasy comedy full of absurdist humor and illogical behavior.

BETWEEN DOG AND WOLF

by Cris Eli Blak

2M, 1W, DRAMA

WINNER OF THE 2024 CHARLES M. GRETCHELL NEW PLAY AWARD
High school friends Blake, Patrick, and Mara reunite at a hotel the day before their 10-year reunion. Forever traumatized by the school shooting that took place their junior year, the three try and fail to relive painful memories and heal broken friendships.

VERLASSEN

by Avery Lewis

3M, 2W with additional ensemble roles, DRAMA

A prisoner awaiting his punishment. A pastor seeking vengeance. A survivor searching for peace. All three are looking to one girl, Ida Verlassen, to give them what they're after. As time works against them and revelations are made, Ida must decide who she trusts, and which direction she will choose to go.